MURDA MANSION

MURDA MANSION

A. ALEX COME'

Copyright © 2023 by Alex Come'.

ARPress
45 Dan Road Suite 5
Canton MA 02021
Hotline: 1(888) 821-0229
Fax: 1(508) 545-7580

Ordering Information:
Quantity sales. Special discounts are available on quantity purchases by corporations, associations, and others. For details, contact the publisher at the address above.

Printed in the United States of America.

ISBN-13:   Softcover   979-8-89330-851-8
           eBook   979-8-89330-853-2
           Hardcover   979-8-89330-852-5

Library of Congress Control Number: 2024902794

TABLE OF CONTENTS

CHAPTER ONE

It was a blind man's kind of darkness. Thunder rumbled and lightening flashed. Riley McCaden stood alone shivering from the cold, relentless hammering rain.

Truthfully it wasn't just the rain causing him to shiver, there was something else, something very wrong, something he should never have let happen. And now because of it, here he was, alone, with someone, or something, waiting for him here in the thick darkness.

Riley wanted to run, turn and race as hard as he could to safety, to bring back help, bring back an Army! But he could not! He had to face this alone. He had given his word, promised!

The cold rain stung like small lead pellets, soaking into his clothing, and flattening his hair. A chilling wind pushed hard against him. There was no moon or stars to be seen, only rain, wind, and darkness... and one other thing he couldn't shake; the overwhelming fear this was going to be his last day on earth.

Lightening streaked the night sky, filling his world with four seconds of brilliant light...his soul shuddered with terror; the old Mansion beamed with devilish evil...a structural giant, towering, radiating a strange visual warning, a soundless scream of advice...RUN, McCaden, DON'T LOOK BACK...RUN, RUN fast and *NEVER NEVER RETURN!* Then darkness came back..

Thoughts ran wild in Riley's mind. He swallowed hard. Everybody feared this place, this long abandoned Mansion; this antique cadaver old-timers called: *Evil Murda Mansion*. Yes, it had once been a beautiful home, a grand estate, a proud structure made of Oak and Steel and imported Marble, two stories of luxurious living with a grand balcony and terracotta roofing. It was a... Lightening flashed again suddenly, and Riley jump; then darkness came again. Riley's thoughts took a different course.

There were a lot of abandoned houses in Lafayette, but not like this one, this one was different from the others, and not just because of its rotting wooden floors, sagging walls and ceilings. Not because of its loosening marble slabs, weakening roof with occasional sliding tiles, or its many broken out windows.

No! Somewhere along its hundred- and forty-year history, old Murda Mansion had become what many of the old-timers claimed to be a living entity, that somehow, something from another dimension had slipped inside its walls, and in some way, somehow took possession. The old structure remained abandoned of human life, from the outside it looked dead...but life, some odd, dark kind of life lived within its walls! And it was an evil life!

Every kid in town was forbidden to go near it. The old-timers believed it possessed a dark soul; that it lived and breathed, and a pair of hidden eyes watched every step of those foolish enough to come near it. And somehow, in some strange, wicked way, the old building had managed to survive, avoiding destruction at the hands of good God-Fearing men.

And now, standing at its doorstep knowing he had to enter into its dark interior, Riley pondered one very disturbing question...were the stories of what lay waiting beyond the old mansion's door factual? Was its grisly legend true?

According to local accounts, it had all taken place on a night just like tonight: dark and raining and cold. "MURDA MANSION," Riley's lips whispered the words weakly. No way did he want to, he possessed not even one once of desire to; but there was no getting around it. He had to go inside!

CHAPTER TWO

Lightening flashed again. The building glistened. Then darkness.

Standing there in the yard, rain continuing to soak into his clothes, Riley wrapped his arms around his shoulders and rubbed for warmth.

The temperature felt as if he were standing in the frozen glaciers of Alaska. And he felt so alone. Afraid too; he could admit it. Who knew what lay beyond that door? Again thunder rumbled. Lightening followed and again darkness.

The storm was worsening, and he had to get out of it; standing in the open yard made him a perfect target for the lightening. Having brought a flashlight he now switched it on and raised the beam to the mansion's front door.

It would be unlocked; of that he was certain. For Bowdie, his best friend, was in that house somewhere. 'I'll make sure the door's unlocked.' he had promised, 'just in case something happens, and I don't come back.' Riley sputtered a run of water out of his mouth. Well his best friend did not come back. So now here he stood, amid the lightening and rain and cold, carrying out what they had called, *plan B search and rescue*- to enter the old mansion and search for him. Although at the time, neither believed it would ever come to this.

Thunder rumbled through the woods behind him. Riley sighed shaking his head. It was time! Trudging his way to the edge of the front porch he climbed the steps, "I don't want to do this", he whispered into the loud hammering rain, "God, you know I really don't want to do this." But far too quickly he was there, face to face with the door; although to him it was more than that, it was the entranceway to the Devil's lair.. and this was no Disney World amusement park attraction.

Angry with his best friend for putting him in this situation, he made a face, "Bowdie" he said to himself, *best friend or not, you're a Jackass.*" Riley quickly raised his eyes toward heaven, "sorry Lord, I know it's wrong to call people names and I'm struggling with it. But even you must admit when it comes to girls that is exactly what Bowdie is. And I know you saw him enter through this door, and never came out. Now, because of plan ' B', I may not either!"

All of this was happening because of Bowdie falling for Michaela Warrington, the new girl in school. Having arrived straight from Sydney, Australia, Riley had to admit, she was unquestionably a scorcher and her accent turned up the heat. Every guy in school drooled like a Pavlov dog when she'd walk past. And of all the guys she had to choose from, it was Bowdie, his best friend that she picked.

Riley made another face. And Michaela choosing him was conditional: that he prove his worthiness by sneaking into old Murda Mansion at exactly midnight and spray-paint her name in big letters on one of the walls, in a location where it could be seen looking safely through an outside window. Riley shook his head whispering with gritted teeth, *Bowdie! Bowdie! Bowdie!*

Reaching out, he gripped the door handle, turning it slowly. And following one long deep breath he pushed. The wooden giant swung inward, crying out; its loud moaning seeming to drown out the wind and hammering rain. Riley's brain screamed at him not to go in. But he forced himself not to listen.

The beam from his flashlight streaked into the interior, into what appeared a large living room. And just as the old stories told, its furniture lay scattered and broken. And now following all those years of neglect it lay covered with mildew and rotting. The smell was disgusting.

Spider webs were everywhere. Riley thought of Bowdie again. His best friend hated spiders, suffered from Arachnophobia, an uncontrollable fear of the insect. To Bowdie, the only good spider was one with its blood and guts streaked across the floor.

As Riley stood staring into the darkness beyond the doorway, his thoughts shifted again, this time to the cold murky loneliness of outer space. There was no telling what lay beyond the beam of his flashlight; it could be anything, all sorts of hideous and unspeakable things, and here in Murda Mansion, like space, no one would hear him scream.

Squeezing his eyes tight Riley told himself, *"Zip it McCaden, it doesn't freaking matter anyway."* He looked up again and whispered, *"Sorry God!"*

CHAPTER THREE

Riley took one long step and was through the door. He stopped and stood waiting…for something! But nothing happened. He took two more steps, still nothing.

Outside, the rain continued hammering the ground and exploding into the countless puddles of water; its loud roar rushing through the open doorway behind him. Riley fought to remain calm, resisting an escalating panic. His senses told him once again to get out, that something was in this house; and it wasn't Bowdie he was thinking about.

What if the Legend was true? he thought. What if the old timers were right? That Murda's ghost did haunt this old place? Could it be here right now, watching? Laughing?

Lightening flashed, the interior dimly illuminated, then quickly went black.

Riley grew angry at himself again, whispering aloud. "Come on McCaden, there are no such things as Ghosts."

Lightening flashed again, then darkness. He really, really wanted to go home. But he just couldn't. This place, this…thing, was holding his best friend somewhere inside and was never intending to let him go. Like it or not, he had to continue, he had to find Bowdie. Casting the beam of his light throughout the room, Riley's mind recalled the legend of Murda Mansion.

Everyone knew the story. It had happened on a night just like this one. Judge Murda had made countless enemies back in those days; often sending innocent people to prison for long periods of time. And if he wasn't putting them behind bars, he was ordering them hung at the giant Oak Tree near the edge of the woods. It was said he never missed a hanging. That always he would sit in his horse drawn buggy just beyond the crowd, smoking a long cigar and wearing a grin of self-satisfaction.

Because so many had met their end at that tree, he was given a most befitting nickname… 'The Old Neck Stretcher'. But one fateful night in 1891 he did however, meet with a horrible end himself.

Hundreds of people had come from all around, angry and seeking revenge. Guided by the light of burning torches they formed a massive circle around the house, demanding he come out and face them. Throughout the crowd they chanted his name over and over… "Murda - Murda - Murda - Murda! But some say the word they chanted wasn't Murda at all, that it was actually… "Murderer - Murderer - Murderer."

Terrified, the Judge refused to go out. Instead, he ran and hid, covering his ears to their horrible chanting. Angered that he would not face them, several of the men broke into the house and began searching for him. Tempers wild, they destroyed nearly everything in their paths, tipping over furniture and breaking mirrors, scattering books, and flipping tables. They kicked open doors, looked under beds, dumped the contents of drawers on the floor, and even pulled wallpaper from the walls. Their search continued endlessly until finally, they found him huddled behind a pile of boxes in the attic.

Caught up in their mad desire for revenge, the angry men swung a rope over the attic rafters and tightened it around Murda's neck. And there, on that very night, the old Judge was hung to death in his own house, while the heartless crowd outside waved their torches chanting the name they so hated… "Murda-Murda-Murda!"

Riley swallowed. It didn't end there. According to legend his body was left hanging and never taken down. The old mansion was sealed up and never entered again. Until now!

CHAPTER FOUR

A sudden crack of thunder caused Riley to jump. Again he thought about Bowdie. Where in this house could he be? Was he okay? Surely he wasn't…D.E.A.D. Riley spelled the word to himself, afraid to even say it under his breath. Sometimes just saying something out loud could somehow make it come true.

How could anyone come here in the first place? Rolling his eyes Riley said the word instantly: MICHEALA! What a manipulator, he thought. Obviously he had been brought up so differently than she. In his family they were taught to treat others nice and with respect.

Still, Riley had to blame himself for some of this too. It was he who had convinced his parents to let him and Bowdie campout in the tent in the backyard. Otherwise, there would have been no way for Bowdie to sneak away and do Michaela's ridiculous bidding.

Thinking about it, Riley grew annoyed with himself. In a way, he had lied to his mom and dad; that was wrong, and he knew it. Yet, Bowdie was his best friend and that had put him in the middle. The right thing to do would have been to tell Bowdie no, that he would not deceive his parents. Now, because he had, Bowdie was missing; and soon, he might be too.

Another whip of lightening illuminated the room; horror sucked the breath out of Riley's lungs, his breathing stopped, he nearly screamed. On the far wall through an arched doorway, a long willowy shadow appeared; the shadow of a man; a man holding something long and pointed.

Darkness came again. The room filled with blackness; a burst of thunder rumbled. Then it fell quiet again except for the falling rain. Riley fought to keep his wits about him…*Get a grip! Get a grip!* He pointed the beam of his light through the archway and onto the far wall…nothing was there, it was gone.

He whispered, his head shaking, "I'm in deep Critical Crap." Chewing on his bottom lip he stared thoughtfully. If his parents had been there they'd be yelling at him. They hated it when he chewed on his lip, fearing he'd be gnawing on it one of these days and when something terrible happened, he'd bite a chunk right out of it.

But that was the least of his problems. The question right now was what should he do? No, he told himself angrily; it's what *you should have done.* You should have told dad everything and brought him here with you. NOW, you may not live long enough to even see him again.

Riley hated himself. Actually, bottom-line, going to his Dad had never been an option. Bowdie had made him promise that if something happened, no one would come searching but he alone. And he had given his word.

His thoughts shifted to Prissy, Missy Michaela. Actually, what he should have done was drag her butt down here with him and let her get the daylights scared out of her and not just have to look through a window.

Riley imagined Michaela standing beside him now, clinging like poison ivy to a tree. He shook his head. Actually he was thankful she wasn't along; this was no place for a girl anyway. She'd have begun screaming long ago and still not have run out of air. Like it or not, he admitted, Bowdie was his best friend, and it was his responsibility alone to find him.

Cold wind continued howling in through the open door behind. Riley realized his teeth were chattering. He'd have paid a million dollars for a change of dry clothes and a warm sweater. But that wasn't going to happen, not until he found Bowdie.

So biting at his bottom lip again he sighed, and with great reluctance began moving deeper into the unknown darkness of Murda Mansion; on toward the doorway of the room where he had seen that shadow. *The shadow,* he thought, likely it had been nothing more than an allusion, a trick of the mind...but what if it wasn't?

Inching along, Riley thought about his dad. He wasn't here beside him physically, but he was there in spirit. Chewing hard on his lip, Riley thought about something his Dad had once told him a long time ago. Something he was now truly beginning to understand. His dad had told him, ' the biggest part of growing up was learning to face your fears'.

CHAPTER FIVE

Riley was scared. But what could he do, Bowdie was in trouble, and he had given his word. Light from the flashlight helped ease his nerves a little, but at the same time brought a shiver of added fear. Was the beam dimmer now than when he had first come through the door? He tapped the light against his other hand. *Come on, brighten.* The batteries couldn't be going dead already. Not this soon.

Each step Riley took moved him farther away from the outdoors, his safety zone. Lightening flashed again then dark. Strangely he thought of the old Judge. Lifting his eyes he stared into the darkness above. Was the old neck stretcher still up there? Were his bones still hanging just as the legend says?

Thunder rumbled somewhere to the north. Riley sighed and pulled his eyes back to the narrow area lighted by the flashlight. He hated Murda Mansion. By far, this was the most frightful thing he had ever had to do. And as he grew closer to the room ahead, he thought more and more about that shadow.

Shifting his beam he glanced at his watch; 2:16 am, still a long while before daylight. Thinking once again about Bowdie, he let his thoughts shift to the events leading up to his presence here.

Bowdie had left the tent at exactly 11:30 pm, acting cool and not at all afraid…he was full of it; even The Rock himself would think twice before coming here alone.

His best friend was supposed to have been back no later than 1:00pm, giving him an hour and a half to walk here, sneak in, and paint Michaela's name on the wall. Then get back. But he never returned. What had happened that he never came out of this house?

Riley pulled a glob of cobwebs from his face. He felt something crawling near his ear and brushed it away. Outside, the hammering rain was beginning to ease, slowing to a drizzle. But the wind remained loud and harsh.

His mind shifted to the shadow. It was probably nothing more than his imagination – but if it wasn't, than whom or what was it?

And what was the object the shadow had been holding? Or worse, what if it wasn't a shadow at all? What if it was Murda's ghost? Riley shook his head. It couldn't have been the Judge. He would have been floating, not standing still like a man; that is if ghosts really do exist. Riley made a face. *Stop it you idiot?*

But his mind wouldn't let him; if the shadow had been a real live person, than somebody was in here with him; somebody besides Bowdie. His best friend might think of himself as cool, collected, and invincible, but he'd never stay in this horrible place this long, not if he had a choice.

Riley shook his head. With his luck, the shadow-man was probably an escaped convict, or run-a-way crazy man from an insane asylum; some unshaven, bad-breathed murdering nutcase calling this place home; living on rats, cockroaches and drinking rainwater. Riley yelled at himself, *will you freaking quit*. But he just couldn't.

There were dozens of possibilities. And what worried him most was the object the shadow had been holding. Was it a sword, a razor-sharp knife stretched long by the trickery of shadows, a baseball bat, a tire iron, or maybe an old ash covered Poker from the antique fireplace? All would make the perfect murder weapon. Riley bit down hard on his lip, hoping the pain would chase away his continuing toddler-mentality. It didn't.

As if yelled by a Marine Corp Drill Instructor Riley's mind shouted, "Halt". Immediately he stopped, almost coming to attention. Lightening blitzed the room but quickly went dark.

He was at the archway! *Face your fear, McCaden!*

Hoping for a surge of courage he told himself repeatedly: *face your fear, face your fear, face your fear!* No surge came. What if that shadow did belong to a killer, a serial killer? What if he was waiting there right now, hidden in all that darkness? What if he was like what's his name, that murderer who ate people and stored their remaining body parts in 55 gallon drums?

Riley didn't want to die, especially here in this old mansion where he may never be found. Chewing on his lip again, his mind went self-destructive; he couldn't stop it... he imagined his dead body lying on the old kitchen table sawed into pieces; the killer wearing a chef's hat while frying one of his hands in a sauce pan seasoned with salt, pepper, and a sprinkle of paprika.

He was just one step, only one step from being horribly murdered and eaten for breakfast. Oh how he dreaded crossing into that room. Yet, what choice did he have? What if that's where Bowdie was? More than ever he wished his dad were with him. Truthfully, at this point, he'd have settled for his mom. Heck, he'd even consider Michaela; maybe her screaming would scare the killer away.

Continuing to chew on his lip, Riley stood teetering at the doorway. To go in, or not to go in, that was the question? Actually, he yelled at himself, that was not the question. It wasn't even a matter of question. It was a matter-of-fact. He had to go in.

CHAPTER SIX

Outside the mansion, the storm continued with its drizzling rain, booming thunder, and flashes of light. The wind howled angrily through the open door. It pushed through the mansion's shattered windows moaning and howling through the dark, rushing through the lonely rooms and long dark hallways.

Riley thought of its howling as music: Dark, Eerie, Disturbing Music, a spooky melody floating into this world, into this house, streaming from some evil-dimensional instrument; an altered Pipe-Organ perhaps, with twisted, disfigured pipes possessing huge eyes and laughing mouths. And he knew just who the Musician would be: The Grim-Reaper himself. And the title of his song…*Get Out You Idiot!*

Riley chewed on his lip like a machine gun spitting bullets. Standing there at the arched doorway, his conscious argued with his subconscious. "Man, you don't have to do this. You don't have to go into that room. *Yes. I do!* No you don't. *Yes I do. Bowdie might be in there.* He might not too. Run and get help. *NO!* Do you want to die? *I'm not going to die. Shadow man isn't even real.*" Yes he is, you numskull, you saw him. He's in there right now waiting to kill, cook and eat you. *Shut up.* No, you shut up and listen."

Spontaneously Riley whispered, *'God please let me go to Heaven'*, then he stormed into the room and stopped. Motionless he waited with eyes clamped tight. He wasn't sure what he waited for: maybe something to come crashing down against his head and crush his skull or the pain of that long-pointed object being thrust through his body ripping through his heart and lungs and guts.

But nothing happened! Slowly Riley opened one eye, then the other. The room remained dark and quiet, except for the wind. Flashlight gripped tightly, he raised its beam and scanned the area. The room was massive.

Paintings and pictures covered the walls, although many hung crooked, others lay smashed in pieces on the floor. Furniture lay disarrayed, tipped over or broken. Far to the left, Riley's light caught the corner of a giant mirror. It was a dull reflection, but the slow movement of the beam showed it running full length of the wall, ceiling to floor. It was monstrous. The dim light also showed cracks in several places.

In his mind Riley imagined the night they had come for the Judge. He could almost hear the shouts of the angry crowd and see the burning torches outside the windows. In his imagination his ears echoed their chant. He could picture the enraged men here inside, tipping over furniture and throwing objects angrily against the mirror. So eerie was the feeling, he could almost hear the breaking of the glass.

Shaking his head, he chased away those images by focusing on the mirror's beauty. Aside from the cracks, it was still totally intact. In the upper left-hand corner, part of the frame had come loose and now hung arched over its face. Riley wondered where such a mirror had come from in those days.

Lightening flashed; the room lit up. There was no stopping Riley's scream. The terrifying reflection of shadow-man was there in the mirror, he was right behind him, only inches away, towering high over his head. The lightening died and darkness took over the room.

Riley was sure he had crapped in his pants. He wanted to run but his legs wouldn't move, besides, the madman was too close. There was no hope for escape. So there in the blackness, his scream echoing through the dark interior of Murda Mansion he waited, wondering what instrument the killer would use: the Sword, the Knife, the Bat or Poker.

He had heard it said that in the final moments just before you die; your life flashes before you. It was true. His mind sent fleeting images of nearly everyone he had ever known: his mom, dad, Bowdie, aunts, uncles, cousins, neighbors, cat, dog, and Michaela…. **Michaela!**

Seconds ticked past. But the end of his life never came. The man who stood behind him remained motionless. Why? Why wasn't Shadow man murdering him?

Riley's scream finally faded, and the mansion's darkness gave way to the sounds of wind and rain. Not moving, flashlight spotting the floor, Riley asked himself: dare I move? Was that what this killer-cannibal wanted? Was he playing with him, making sport of ending his life?

Minutes passed and neither of them moved. It had become a stalemate. Someone needed to do something. Riley thought about another thing his dad had once said. A man should always try and do the right thing, but if the time comes when he's not sure what to do, he needs to do something even if it's wrong. Again Riley thought it best to trust his dad. Slowly, ever so slowly, he turned to face the killer behind him.

This was it. Would the big man finally end the game? Had this been the way it was for Bowdie? Had this towering giant been his best friend's executioner? Was Bowdie's lifeless body lying in this very room?

Riley had now turned completely and was facing the taunting psycho. Inch at a time he dragged the beam of his light up to the killer's face when there he gasped. Within the flashlight's dim glow Riley McCaden stood stunned, shocked, and speechless.. Who would have ever guessed?

Raising his free hand, Riley tapped shadow-man's chest with his knuckles. The heavy metal breastplate clanged beneath the blow…A SUIT OF ARMOR! An old suit of Armor, holding a long spear in a medal gloved hand.

Not a man at all! No killer, no insane person, no American Cannibal, and for sure no ghost. Then reality hit home and Riley thought, *OH NO!* Although the medal had clanged when he tapped it, it could be that someone, or something still stood waiting inside the armor remaining motionless, smug, and grinning, just waiting for the last laugh...excited over Riley's murder and then comes the barbecue.!

Riley knew he had to look, had to make sure, had to know. Slowly, his hand both cold and shaky, reached up until it rested on the face shield. Pausing briefly, he took a deep breath; then pushed it up. The beam of his flashlight shimmered into the interior. Riley held the light there as if frozen. He was ready to scream...but didn't! Closing his eyes he sighed. NOTHING! EMPTY! A giant expression of relief showed on Riley's face.

Glancing up into the darkness again, he whispered out loud, "Oh thank you Lord, thank you, thank you.

Turning back to the big open room he shined his light off into the darkness ahead, continuing with his whispering, "Well God, I know it was wrong to call Bowdie a Jack you know what. But right now I feel like one myself. So out of respect, I'll just say this…I am for sure a Donkey."

CHAPTER SEVEN

Careful of the scattered furniture strewn about, Riley moved away from shadow-man and deeper into the black core of the mansion, into a third room. It was here he found something he didn't want to find. Something that sent shivers down his spine. Something that would prove more fearful than anything he had yet faced.

He had found the landing of a great stairway going up. Riley didn't want to go up. Going up would mean finding the Attic. Up there it was for sure darker than space. All of his life adults had been saying darkness was nothing to be afraid of. Easy for them, they had never been alone in Murda Mansion.

The stairway that lay in front of him was wide, its steps covered with thick, dark carpeting. The flashlight was little help, but it did, although dull, show the giant staircase winding its way up to the distant light-less world of the top floor. Above that would be the frightful attic.

Resembling a hotel, there were a line of rooms on the floor. Was Bowdie in one of them? Pausing at the bottom of the stairs, Riley remained still, contemplating his next move.

A crack of thunder sounded. This whole thing was crazy. What was he doing here alone anyway? He needed to break his word and go get his dad. Better still, call the Police. After all, Bowdie had disappeared, that made him a missing person. And if he himself remained, he may very well end up the same way; then neither of them might never be found.

Riley sighed with frustration. Like it or not, he couldn't do that. He had promised, given his word, sworn on an oath that only he would come if something happened. Besides, in the McCaden family there had always been an understanding that other than your faith in God, nothing was more important than keeping your word. A man's promise was the value of his life; another thing his dad had taught him. "Yeah Dad," Riley whispered into the darkness, "the value of my life…or as it may be, the value of my death!"

There was another noiseless flash of lightening, and it gave him a lighted glimpse of the dreadful place waiting above. Doors hung half off their hinges, sections of railing were missing. Old wallpaper dangled to the floor, and like below, pictures and paintings hung crooked or missing.

In some places there were large holes in the walls through which thin slabs of wood protruded like reaching fingers. There appeared more cobwebs than below as well. And for the entire stretch of wall running all the way up to the landing, the wall seemed to be moving. Riley frowned, then sighed. *Cockroaches, thousands of dirty, germ carrying, scurrying cockroaches. Moving North, South, East, and West, over top of each other non-stop.*

He did not want to go up. There were countless areas downstairs where Bowdie could be. But it was here at the stairway he stood. Was it destiny? Was he meant to go up? He had moved through three rooms in a straight line from the front door and this is where he ended up. It had to be fate, or perhaps God's will for him.

So, careful not to touch the railing or wall, Riley placed his foot on the first step, took a deep breath and started his climb. The steps creaked, many felt weak and rotted beneath the old dust covered carpet. In several spots they sagged and felt as though they might break through. He moved quickly off those and onto another.

Nearly halfway to the first floor his eye caught a glimpse of something that stopped him cold. Bending, he lowered his light for a closer look.

Imprinted within the thick film of dust was a single set of footprints. BOWDIE! Riley smiled with hope.

If any doubts existed that Bowdie had never made it to Murda Mansion; they now disappeared. His best friend had definitely been here. He had climbed these very steps. And although it made Riley feel a little better, he now found himself considering two questions: why his best friend had gone upstairs, and more importantly, why hadn't he come down. The tracks were a one-way trip up!

CHAPTER EIGHT

Sighing, Riley shook his head. This had been the longest night of his life. He wanted so much to just find Bowdie and go home. Based on the one-way tracks, he wondered if someone had been up there waiting, and when Bowdie reached the top they grabbed him. If that had been the case, then somewhere in this house there were another set of stairs, another way of coming and going.

Riley ran his fingers through his hair, reasoning. If someone had kidnapped Bowdie, where did they take him, and why would they even want him? Bowdie was a scholar-brain in school, but limited in skills like taking out the trash, mowing the grass and washing the car when he was suppose too. And when it came to cleaning his room his mom and dad had too threaten his life. Other than his family loving him, and being his best friend, Bowdie would prove little value to anyone else.

Yes, there were cases of people being kidnapped and taken to foreign countries; human trafficking they called it, modern day slavery. That could have been the case, but not likely. Bowdie and he both felt strongly about the injustice of slavery during the Civil War, especially Bowdie, being African American. Had that been the reason for his being kidnapped, he'd have begun a campaign of lecturing and resisting to the point of driving them mad. It had to be something else, but what?

Again Riley pulled his light down to the footprints; a new thought was popping in his head. What if the tracks weren't Bowdie's? To be sure, he lifted his own foot and placed it inside one of the prints. Fear struck like the blow from a baseball bat to the chest. The print was bigger… definitely not Bowdie's. These belonged to a man, a fully grown man. Riley quickly shut off his light and listened. Just what he was listening for he wasn't sure. All he knew was that someone, a grown adult, had climbed this staircase and not that long ago.

Slowly Riley turned his eyes to the top of the blackened stairs. Was that someone still in this house? If so, where were they hiding, or perhaps a better way of putting it, where were they waiting?

For several minutes he stood in the darkness with ears alert. Once again he was faced with a decision. Should he make a run for it, or continue on and stay true to his promise? Once more his dad's words came to mind, 'a man's promise was the valuable of his life'. Riley was realizing decisions were not always easy, and more than ever he respected his parents for all the ones they had to make in life.

Shrugging, he sighed and switched his light back on. The beam shot to the top of the stairs. *If you can't trust your dad, who can you trust?* Once again he started up. But in less than two steps he stopped suddenly, his eyes widening. Something was crawling quickly up his legs, over his neck and into his hair… COCKROACHES!"

Wildly, Riley brushed at his head and began wiggling madly to try and shake the insects free from his skin. They covered his clothes. The dirty little things were hanging on tight, scampering about, exploring, searching, probing his body for even a morsel of food. They were inside his clothing running everywhere over his body. He wanted to scream but didn't dare for fear the stranger in the house might hear.

One of the insects ran across his cheek and he slapped it, guts splattered the side of his face. Another started in his ear but came right back out. In a wild frenzy, Riley slammed down the flashlight and ripped off his shirt using it as a brush. He unbuckled his pants and dropped them to his ankles, then pulled them off along with his sneakers. Again he used his shirt as a brush, sending the nasty insects flying. For everyone he knocked free, it felt a dozen more scurried over his skin somewhere.

He should have never paused on the stairway. Frantically he brushed and swiped, sending them flying through the air like blades of grass from a weed-cutter, but the fight seemed endless. They never bit, but they nibbled at his skin, hungry, starving, determined to find food. The feel of their nasty legs sent shivers down his spine.

Riley wanted to run, but where could he go. He was trapped on a stairway, forced to stand his ground and fight…man against insect. And fight he did. Like a flag in the wind his shirt moved savagely, brushing, and striking, knocking them free. It had become a bitter battle. They had challenged him, pushed him in a corner, riled him, given him the creeps, forced him to fight; a fight he was determined to win…and win he did.

After what seemed an endless amount of time slinging and slapping, he finally stood alone on the stairs. His chest was heaving, his face sober and he stood only in his underwear and socks. Motionless he remained quiet, waiting for the feel of their crawling legs, but there were none. All had lastly been killed or sent flying.

Recovering his pants he shook them then began to dress. When finished he grabbed the light and hurried along, moving once again toward the top of the stairway. He hated Murda Mansion.

CHAPTER NINE

Nearly every step creaked beneath Riley's weight. If sneaking past someone ever become a plan for escape, taking the stairs was out. You'd have to be a weightless ghost to not be heard. Riley thought of the old Judge.

Was his ghost real? Maybe it was. He had watched a lot of documentaries on the existence of ghosts and spirits. There were scores of witnesses who confessed to seeing them; many were reputable people. If Murda was here now, was he watching, hovering just above his head maybe, laughing. And what would he look like, feel like, act like? Would he be able to talk? Could those footprints on the stairs be his? Riley felt the step beneath him start to break and jumped quickly to the next one.

Ghosts he thought to himself. Yeah, maybe! But Vampires, Aliens, Werewolves, and all the other movie monsters, they were nothing more than creations born out of human imagination. Of that he was sure. *Well, pretty sure…hopefully sure.*

In Health he had learned it was often difficult for the human mind to distinguish between reality and make-believe; that made sense. Having thought Shadow-man was a serial killer was a good example. An empty harmless suit of armor had made him scream like a little child fearing the boogie man. *What a moron.*

From this moment on he would act more like an adult. In fact, if it were possible he'd gladly trade both his XBOX and life- size poster of Christina Aguilera just to become one. And the choice he'd become would be The Rock. Pausing a moment, Riley made a thoughtful face, than raised one of his eyebrows… *maybe not trade the poster; Christina was older yes, but she was a WOW! And her music was mind-blowing.*

Having reached the top of the stairs Riley stepped onto the first floor. Pausing, he shined his light down the long dark walkway. Many of the doors angled oddly, hanging partly off their hinges. Others stood open or closed.

Every room would have to be checked. Bowdie could be tied and gagged in any one of them; just waiting to be freed. Then again, the man who had left those tracks on the stairway could be here too.

Riley made his way to the first room. The door was closed. Lightening flashed and bathed it in a split second of light. Like the front door, this one was big, towering high over his head. The top was rounded, and it appeared wider than normal, resembling the door of an old English Castle. Then darkness filled the mansion again.

Reaching through the beam of the flashlight Riley gripped the handle and turned, it clicked softly. He felt the door give. Swallowing, he bit hard on his lip. The only thing left now was to push it open. He hoped more than anything Bowdie was in there waiting.

Riley pushed. The door squeaked, opening wider and wider until striking the inside wall with a soft thud. The beam from his flashlight shot into the room. He could make out the shape of an old bed; the kind with four posts and a canopy over top. There was a window to the right and just as he spotted it, lightening flashed. For a second, he caught a glimpse of the tree tops in the distance. Just a short walk beyond those trees home was waiting. But it may as well have been a thousand miles away.

The room went dark again. Carefully Riley moved farther in, always making sure nothing lay in his path that might trip him. He found a dresser, a small closet, an old trunk at the foot of the bed, and a small table and chair in one of the corners. But no Bowdie!

Disappointed, he turned to leave when his ears picked up a sound that didn't belong. Immediately he switched off his light and crouched beside the bed. Panic rose. The sound that shouldn't have been there was moving in his direction. He recognized it; for he too had made it himself. It was the creaking of the stairway. Someone was coming!

CHAPTER TEN

Whoever it was coming up the stairs, they were big. He could tell by the loud creak of the steps. So for certain it wasn't Bowdie. Could it be the same man who had already made those prints in the dust; coming up now to search for him, to hunt him down and take him to where they held Bowdie? Or worse, do to him what they had already done to his best friend - whatever horrible thing that might be.

But on the bright side, maybe it was his dad! Riley frowned. Yeah right! The way his luck was going it was probably the Old Neck Stretcher in search of a victim, someone to murder and change into a ghost like himself. After well over a hundred and twenty years he was probably starving for company. Riley shook his head, *Man you better lay off the Stephen King novels and movies.*

The squeaking noise fell suddenly silent! Riley caught his breath. The person had paused on the steps for some reason. HIS TRACKS! That had to be it. They had discovered his footprints the same way he had discovered theirs. Riley pictured them bent over staring with cold, suspicious eyes. Now they would know for sure he was in the house.

It was all he could do to keep from cursing at the disaster this whole venture was turning out to be. He wondered if there was any such thing as 'good luck'.

Realizing his thoughts were drifting, he shook his head forcing his mind back to the now. Through the darkness came a new sound: VOICES. Two men talking softly; discussing something he couldn't quite make out. He shook his head again. *Great! Two people were looking for him now.*

Impatiently Riley leaned forward hoping to hear a little more clearly. Then the creaking started again, and he knew instantly they had started back up the steps in his direction.

Crouched beside the bed he wasn't sure what to do. The approaching men reached the top of the stairs and stepped onto the landing. There they paused once more. This time Riley watched as a beam of light shot into the darkness past the open door. Then almost immediately it came back to shine at an angle into the very room where he waited. He gasped, *"Crap!"*

The two men spoke again, this time close enough for him to hear every word. One had a very deep voice and reminded him of a Bull Frog. It was as though the man croaked every word rather than speak it. Maybe it was more like a grunt, he thought. The other man's voice was higher pitched. Nervously Riley listened to their conversation. "Is that the room?" The man with the reptilian voice asked.

"First floor, first door, that's what he told us, Frog." The high-pitched voice told him.

Riley bit at his lip, repeating the name high-pitched voice man had used. 'FROG', it fit the voice. He wondered if it would fit the face too. Then they began moving again, heading straight to the room where he remained crouched. The beam from their light bounced on the wall of the bedroom as they approached.

Throwing himself flat, Riley rolled twice and was under the bed just as the two stepped through the doorway. Their light streaked everywhere for several seconds before anything was said. Riley held his breath thinking, *don't look under the bed. Don't look under the bed. Please don't let them look under the bed.*

"There it is Harvey" the one named Frog croaked.

Riley watched as the beam from their flashlight fell on the old trunk. They were after the trunk, not him! Silently he sighed. Then came more conversation. "I'll tell you Frog," the high-pitched man called Harvey said, "I'll be so glad when we're out of this place. It gives me the creeps. I hate these old houses, and this one is haunted."

Frog snickered. "You're spineless, Harvey. None of the others are scared. And for crying out loud you're carry a gun."

"Yeah, but guns don't kill things that are already dead."

Frog laughed. "Speaking of creeps, did you take care of that nosy black kid?" Riley's ears perked up…they had to be referring to Bowdie! Both men crouched and grabbed an end of the trunk. Both groaned as they stood, then shuffled out the door with it. Their light grew dimmer as they moved.

Harvey gave Frog his answer, "Yeah, just like you ordered. Drug the smart mouth to the attic and now he's keeping the old man company?"

CHAPTER ELEVEN

The glow from their flashlight quickly vanished and darkness returned to the room where Riley lay. For several minutes he didn't move. He felt safe beneath the bed and needed time to sort things out. For starters, he knew where Bowdie was now. In the Attic, in the attic with the old man… Murda! So the legend was true.

Plus, they talked about the others not being afraid, which meant more people were in the house somewhere. And the trunk they carried out, what was in it? Both had groaned when they lifted it, so it must have been heavy. Where were they taking it and why?

Riley rolled out from beneath the bed. Leaving his light off, he felt his way to the door and glanced cautiously toward the stairs. The men with the trunk were at the bottom now disappearing into another room.

Once again Riley's thoughts shifted to his best friend, 'in the attic keeping the old man company', that's what they said. *Had they hung Bowdie? Was he up there now, dangling from a rafter beside the old neck-stretcher himself?*

Riley couldn't stop the vision. He pictured the two side by side: the judge a set of old bleached out bones covered with rotting clothes, and Bowdie beside him staring lifeless into the darkness, waiting for his best friend to come and cut him down. Riley's eyes filled with wetness. He couldn't help it. And he couldn't stop the conscious thought troubling his heart: *'what have I caused by deceiving my parents?'*

The Attic! From the very beginning he knew that's where Bowdie would be, up there in that one-man graveyard; now two- man graveyard.

Wiping at his eyes he shook his head; **"NO!** I won't accept it. This is 2023, not 1888." Bowdie was in the attic alright, but he wasn't dead. And they may have hung him - but not by the neck, it would have been by the wrists.

Bowdie Pager was one to speak his mind and setting things straight, so they may have strung him up alright, even put a gag in his mouth, but they would not have done to him what that mob had done to the Judge all those years ago.

Riley clicked on his light, marched to the stairway leading up and began his search for the attic entrance. The floor was the same as down stairs; pictures hung at odd angles, there were cobwebs, cockroaches, wallpaper curled to the floor and flat wooden slats poked through plaster-crumbled holes. Constantly he watched over his shoulder expecting to see the two men called Frog and Harvey storming after him.

He scanned his light along the ceiling in search of a pull-down hatch; he saw none. That meant the way to the attic had to be a set of stairs behind one of the doors. For the first time since venturing into this dreadful place, good luck struck. The first door he opened was it.

A steep stairway rose almost straight up. Hesitating at the base Riley used his fingers to push back hair falling over his eyes. There was light above, something up there was glowing.

He tried making sense of it. The old place had no electricity. Could it be a lantern left burning so Bowdie wouldn't be frightened? He rolled his eyes, *Yeah right, for a kid they called creep.* It had to be something else.

The thought was instant…MURDA! It was his ghost! It made sense. Some forms of spirits radiated light, he had seen it on countless TV specials, read about it; they called the light ectoplasmic energy?

Riley stood chewing on his lip. Maybe they had hung Bowdie after all, and now he was a Ghost just like the old neck-stretcher. Was he seeing their combined ectoplasm energy?

Somewhere in the far distance thunder rumbled. So what if he was a ghost, Riley thought, they were best friends; a best friend ghost wouldn't hurt his best friend still alive.

Still chewing on his lip, he started his climb up the steep steps, asking himself...would he?

CHAPTER TWELVE

Six steps from the top Riley halted briefly. Slowly he raised his head peering out over the attic floor. The room opened into a large unfinished area; and although the light was dull and shadowy, he could make out the bare rafters and darkened peek of the attic's high roof. All sorts of paraphernalia hung from spikes hammered into the wooden walls and beams. Boxes of junk were piled everywhere. It was just as the legend said, plenty of places for Murda to have hidden.

"Okay Riley," he told himself in a whisper, "you're here, now you have to finish what you started." Climbing the last few steps, he found himself standing in the one place he promised himself he'd never come: the legendary loft of the Devil's lair.

Yet here he stood, staring into the dark shadowy edge of his worst nightmare. And in this dream there would be no waking up.

Beads of sweat streaked his face. What he was about to do would make one award-winning episode of the old show Fear Factor. And given the choice of moving deeper into this attic, or eating a bowl of hissing Madagascar cockroaches swimming in a stew of dog vomit, he'd have quickly asked for a spoon and napkin.

Nevertheless this was it, the moment of truth. He would soon know the answer too many questions. He would know of Bowdie's condition, if the bones of the old Judge still hung from the rafters, and whether or not his ghost did in fact haunt the place. He would know the source of the attic's light and learn one more very important thing - if he had the courage to see this thing through. More than ever it was all he could do to not turn and run.

Like with the Suit-of-Armor downstairs, his shadow clung to the wall behind him, tall and willowy. Its dark form looked almost alive, stretching eerily up the wall and partly across the ceiling. And when he moved, it moved too, making Riley feel almost as if it possessed a personality all its own.

Junk lay everywhere. He had entered into a dark cluttered maze. Stacks of boxes and crates formed narrow passageways and thick rafters supported the walls and ceiling surrounding him. His eyes darted wildly. He felt trapped in a dimly lighted labyrinth of evil.

To his right an old, rusted bed frame and dust covered mattress stood leaning against the wall; the mattress was blotted with dark stains and he wondered if maybe they were blood. His eyes took in a lot of things he recognized and some he didn't. There was an old wooden rocking horse with long pointed ears and missing tail. Beyond that sat a dining table with high-back chairs stacked on top and covered by a sheet now yellowed with age.

A huge bundle of rope hung from a giant spike, and beside it stretched a long length of rusty chain covered with cobwebs. He counted three old trunks; two large enough to conceal a body. Riley made a face, *Shut it McCaden!*

There were half a dozen animal traps hanging by their chains. A long-rusted saw hung from its handle and an antique wooden tool box sat beneath it filled with iron tools. The items in Murda's attic were countless; all now antique and probably worth a small fortune.

Riley continued to move through the maze of junk. The attic was stale; nothing was moving, no breeze, no noise, and so far no sign of life. His mind kept returning to Murda. Was he actually here? And his best friend; in what condition would he find him? If Bowdie had in fact been hung, how could he possibly handle the sight of it?

He heard a noise for the first time. Quickly ducking behind a stack of wooden crates he held his breath and listened. It was a whirling sound; more like a faint swish, then a tapping, as though something were being struck against a hard surface. It had lasted only seconds and silence came again.

Here in the attic there were no windows or exits to the outside. He assumed the storm had passed since there was no rain falling or sound of thunder rumbling. Soon his dad would be getting up and checking the tent. When he discovered them missing, he'd become worried, grow angry, make a series of phone calls then in panic begin a search.

The noise Riley heard did not return so he rose and continued. Using the back of his hand he wiped away sweat racing toward his eyes. The room ended and made a turn to the left down another narrow walkway through more junk. The light source was growing brighter. Riley had gone but a short distance when he heard a new noise… A RADIO WAS PLAYING!

The sound was turned low and the music soft. But it was a radio; he recognized the tunes. They were old rock and roll songs. The kind listened to back in the 1960's. Riley thought about Murda again. *Do ghosts listen to music?*

Gnawing on his lip he stood thinking this was it; the time had come. At the end of this walkway, he would finally face what he had not wanted to face, the truth concerning the legend of Murda Mansion. But more importantly, he would know at last the true condition of his closest friend, if he were alive or dead.

Wiping sweat from his eyes again Riley crouched and moved on slowly. The strange noise returned: a whooshing sound then tapping and silence. The music stopped and a woman began talking about the weather.

The end of the narrow passageway drew nearer, and the light grew brighter. Then Riley saw shadows on the wall ahead. They were the dark forms of two people sitting at a table across from one another. The sight of it startled him at first, but he felt relief too, at least they weren't the shadowy figure of two bodies hanging from the rafters.

Running a hand through his damp hair Riley moved slowly and quietly, working his way down the remaining stretch of passageway. He gave thought to his predicament. He knew other people were in this house. The question was: who were they, where were they hiding, and why were they here? He also wondered why Harvey and Frog carried that trunk away. However, most importantly he wanted to know the million-dollar question: why they had kidnapped Bowdie?

CHAPTER THIRTEEN

Reaching the end of the walkway Riley crouched behind an old high-back chair. His view was clear. There were two people alright. And much to his relief, one was Bowdie – very much alive.

His best friend was sitting in a chair on the far side of the table, facing his way. Whoever these people were, they were taking no chances. Not only were Bowdie's hands tied, but they had also bound him to the chair with yellow nylon rope. He looked like an African American Criss Angel, Mind Freak, ready to do an escape stunt.

The other shadow was a man sitting with his back to the passageway. In his hands were a deck of cards. Riley watched and listened as he shuffled them, thumbed the end of the deck to create a swooshing sound then straightened them by tapping the deck against the table. He was playing solitaire.

A lantern sat in the middle of the table. That was the source of light he had believed to be the old Judge. No one in the world, Riley assured himself, would ever know he believed a camping lantern to be a ghost.

Scanning the area Riley hoped to come up with a plan. There wasn't as much junk located here, only a few boxes. For the most part horse equipment made up the contents. Most of it hung on the walls: leather harnesses, halters, bridles, belly straps, bits, wood yokes and the like.

There were also two saddles, each straddling a saw horse. In the far corner beyond the table, a big wooden wagon wheel leaned against the wall. The area looked more like an old country barn than an attic.

What to do? Riley turned away and ran a hand through his hair, thinking. There was simply no more time, he had to do something, and it had to be now.

Peering around the chair he studied the man sitting across from Bowdie. If he could sneak up behind him without being noticed, he might get a swing with the flashlight and knock him unconscious. The flashlight was his dad's from long ago, it was aluminum but reasonably sturdy.

Riley pressed his lips. He had never before struck anyone, more less an adult. He doubted he could do it. Yet, what choice did he have. Wrestling with indecision he chewed vigorously on his lip. Knocking the man out was certainly justified; after all, he had his best friend tied up.

Taking a deep breath Riley made his move, slipping quietly out from behind the chair and into the openness of the room. *I've got to do this! It has to be done.*

Soundless, he crept his way to within a few feet before Bowdie spotted him. Instantly Riley raised a finger to his lips. Bowdie caught on quickly. Turning to the man sitting across from him he began a conversation. "So, what's the name of the card game you're playing?" The man looked up for a brief second then back to his cards, volunteering no answer.

From Riley's view, the man did not look that big. His hair was gray, and he looked thin, almost frail. He wore a brown pullover sweater, despite it being hot, and he sat slightly slumped - all the signs of a really old man. Riley remembered Frog and Harvey's words, 'he's up there with the old man.' Now he knew what they meant. They weren't talking about Murda at all. They had been referring to this person.

Riley was growing less confident. This was somebody's Grandfather! How in the world could he bring himself to strike a grandfather in the head with a flashlight? Frustration mounted. The man's age changed everything. What if the blow killed him? How could he live with himself? Yet it was too late to turn around.

Again Bowdie tried capturing the old man's attention. "Sir," he said raising his voice. "Would you teach me how to play that game? It looks fun."

The old man raised his eyes. "I don't rightly see how, son," he said softly, "you don't appear to have the time, you're all tied up." The old man laughed at what was obviously a joke, but Bowdie's forehead wrinkled. "What?"

Then Riley was there, directly behind the old man. Slowly he raised the medal flashlight. He had a clear swing. I can't do this he told himself; but his conscience argued, *"You have to. Do it McCaden. Do it now!"*

Then the old man spoke without turning around. "Go ahead son," he said in a soft, elderly voice, "bring it down, crack this old man's Mellon." Riley was stunned. How did he know?

Slowly the old man turned in his chair. Riley's arm remained raised, ready to strike. The old man was smiling slightly. A lock of gray hair fell across his forehead and wrinkles covered his face, especially around his eyes. A thin mustache traced along his upper lip. Wire rim glasses sat low on his nose.

"Don't look so surprised, son." He said, "Despite these old ears, I heard you coming long before you even got close. Now why don't you hand that flashlight over to me?" The old man widened his smile extending his hand. Lowering his arm, Riley surrendered the light.

"You may as well pull up a chair and sit a spell". He added. "It's for sure you won't be going anywhere." Riley watched him pick up a two-way radio from the table and speak into it, "Below, Casey here. You better send someone to the attic. We've got another visitor, another boy." As the old man talked Riley pulled a third chair out from the table and sat. The radio in the old man's hands crackled and a voice said someone would be right up.

Riley looked at Bowdie. "You okay?"

"Yeah" Bowdie said with a nod, "Sorry about this. But I knew you'd come."

The old man set the radio down looking at Bowdie. "You two must be pretty good buddies." His eyes turned to Riley. "So tell me young man, will there be any more of you coming?"

Riley didn't answer. He was thinking about something the old man had said: that he and Bowdie wouldn't be going anywhere. Not going anywhere would mean not going home. Did he mean not going home ever?

CHAPTER FOURTEEN

The three sat around the table in silence. Riley studied the old man who had gone back to playing solitaire. He guessed him to be at least sixty. A sport coat hung draped over the back of his chair, and over that hung a shoulder holster. Riley was contemplating making a grab for the gun when Bowdie interrupted his thoughts. "Man, Riley, when your dad finds that tent empty, he'll be triple peed."

Pulling his eyes from the gun, Riley looked at Bowdie. "You can count on it. I'll be graduated college and entering Law School before I'm trusted again."

"Dude," Bowdie said, "all this is my fault. But" he grinned, "you have to admit, Michaela is hot."

Riley shook his head. "You know, sometimes I think you're a freak of nature. Your body isn't made up of seventy percent water like everyone else, its seventy percent testosterone."

Smiling, Bowdie wiggled his eyebrows, "Oh yeah, that's why Michaela wants me. The last thing she told me was…" Bowdie never finished his statement. Two men were approaching from the walkway. For the first time Riley got a look at the men who had carried away the trunk; Frog and Harvey.

The one called Harvey was tall and skinny, reminding him of a pool stick wearing jeans, shirt, boots and a ball cap. Frog was a head shorter but with broad powerful shoulders. His hands were big, cheeks chubby and eyes dark. He had a mean look; one warning you not to cross him. Although beginning to bald, he had thick eyebrows and wide thin lips, all the more reminding Riley of a Frog. A short stubby cigar was clenched between his teeth, and they could smell it. It stunk.

At the table the two stopped beside the old man. Frog stared directly at Riley as he talked, "Mr. Climers wants both of these insects brought to the work area. You're to come along too, Casey."

Staring back at Frog, Riley had a crazy thought. Frog had referred to them as insects. Frogs eat insects! What if he was a cannibal? Riley yelled silently at himself, *Man, you are so lame.*

The fat, cigar smoking man moved his eyes to Bowdie. "Harvey," he said, "untie the smelly black kid, I want to get below, my coffee is getting cold."

Frowning, Bowdie looked quickly at Frog, "Man, were you brought up in a barn. You don't say black anymore. I'm an African American kid."

As Harvey moved around the table Frog leaned over and grabbed Bowdie's cheeks with his huge, fat hand. He squeezed hard, "you run from me again and black won't matter, you'll be the color of dead. There are three things in this world I really hate: rats, cats, and young people. You run again and I promise you the sting of something sharp. Got it?"

Bowdie tried to nod but couldn't. When Frog let go, there were finger prints left on his face. Riley understood now why they had tied Bowdie up.

Single file the five marched out of the attic. Riley and Bowdie both wondered where they were being taken. Frog had said the *work area*. What sort of work area? And too, who was Mr. Climers?

Once below, they were lead through the kitchen to a door leading down into the basement. It was dark so Frog and Harvey turned on flashlights. They descended a wooden stairway ending on a cold dirt floor.

The basement was cluttered just like the attic. Judge Murda must have kept everything he ever possessed.

Maneuvering through the muddle of junk they passed in and out of three dark rooms, coming to a stop at an old brick wall. Frog's light shined brightly against it while one of his fat hands slid over the bricks near the top.

Then out of the darkness came a loud scrapping sound as a section of the wall slid inward, then sluggishly moved to the right and stopped. Bright light spilled from the opening. Riley and Bowdie looked at one another. Both astounded.

CHAPTER FIFTEEN

A variety of sounds emerged from inside the hidden area: the idle of a generator, drills, hammering, the chatter of voices, and the shrill of a saw. Without warning, Frog pushed Riley harshly through the opening causing him to stumble. Bowdie looked up with a snap, "Hey, take it easy."

Pulling the cigar from his mouth he kicked Bowdie in the rear, "Shut up you dirt worm and get in there."

When all were inside, the heavy section of wall slid back into place sealing them in. Now, even if his dad came looking, Riley knew he'd never find them.

When their eyes adjusted to the light Riley and Bowdie found themselves staring at a strange object; a huge sphere constructed of silver medal. Located in the center of the room its smooth surface shimmered beneath the string of Fluorescent lights above. A single row of attached red and blue lights encircled the thing shining steadily. There were no windows, only a small door barely large enough for a man to crawl through. Obviously the object was hollow.

Why, Riley wondered; had they built something so big here in the dark basement of an old mansion. He glanced back at the concealed doorway. Whatever the thing was, it would never fit through the opening. It made no sense.

Riley turned back just as someone stepped in front of him. He and Bowdie looked up at the same instant. A tall distinguished looking man with dark hair graying around the temples and wearing a black, pinstriped suit stood smiling. Instantly Bowdie disliked him. He looked too much like their school principal.

The stranger stared a moment then spoke, "Gentlemen," he said, slipping his hands into his pockets, "I'm Mr. Climers and it appears you've created a problem for yourselves, and me. I have no idea why you are here in Murda Mansion, but you've unfortunately stumbled onto a very hushed undertaking, one that, for fear of sounding melodramatic, may very well change the world as we know it."

Climers glanced back at the sphere behind him. "That beautiful piece of technology," he said turning back to them, "is called a TT-V; it is the only one of its kind. No one in the world knows it exists; that is no one but me, the handpicked crew you see here…and sorry to say, now you two."

Riley's eyes roamed the room. Not counting Mr. Climers, Frog, Harvey, and the old man they called Casey, there were six others, each wearing a white lab coat. Obviously they were technicians, specialists in their own fields; whatever expertise that may be. Looking back to the strange sphere, Riley began chewing on his lip.

Finding the bewildered expressions on Riley and Bowdie's face amusing, Climers chuckled. "Gentlemen," he said, "allow me to clarify. The machine behind me is a vehicle. It's not a car, not a train, or top-secret aircraft; it is none of those things. But it is designed to take you where you want to go, and most of the time, bring you back."

Riley and Bowdie glanced at one another, still baffled. "Still don't get it hey," Climers said, "Well let me say this. For you two, I have some good news and some not so good news. The good news is you're going to get a ride in my shiny little machine, it's going to take you to a place no one living today has ever been."

They looked quickly at one another, both thinking the same thing; *if that was the good news, the bad news would definitely suck.* "The bad news gentlemen," Climers continued with a sigh, "is that your ride will be a one-way trip. So just in case you still haven't figured it out, I'll bring it down to kindergarten level. That machine -"

Bowdie cut Climers off, "KINDERGARDEN LEVEL! Here's what I learned in kindergarten." He started to give Climers the finger, but Riley grabbed his hand.

Ignoring Bowdie, Climers finished his statement, "That magnificent piece of technology behind me is called the TT-V; otherwise known as Time Travel-Vehicle.

CHAPTER SIXTEEN

Riley and Bowdie stared at the man called Mr. Climers. Their thoughts were again running parallel ...*TT-V, TIME TRAVEL-VEHICLE. Impossible! Ridiculous!* Apparently this man really did think them kindergartners.

Yet Climers stood his ground with his face remaining serious. There was a long run of silence. All in the work area had ceased what they were doing and stood watching. Slowly, Riley and Bowdie came to grips with what Climers had just told them, realizing he was serious. The expression on their faces changed from *yeah right,* to, *Oh FREAKING CRAP!*

Ignoring the fear on their faces, Climers turned sharply to Casey. "Take them into the lounge and watch them while we put the final touches on the vehicle. DO NOT let them out of your sight. Got it?"

Casey nodded. "Yes sir."

The lounge was located on the far side of the TT-V. The entrance was all glass so anyone sitting inside could watch the activities as they relaxed. The room was like a small kitchenette with a round, wooden table and four chairs sitting in the middle of the floor. There was a coffee pot, a microwave, refrigerator, sink and several overhead cupboards. There was also an open box of candy-bars on the counter near the sink. On the box was a round orange sticker that read, 25 cents. Bowdie pulled a quarter from his pocket and showed it to Casey. "Mind if I buy a bar?"

The old man motioned with his hand. "Put your money back in your pocket son, it's on me. He looked at Riley, "You too, get over there and pick one out." Both walked to the box and rummaged through it. Bowdie chose a Snickers and Riley a Hershey with almonds. They were starving and knew the candy would hit the spot. Back at the table the three sat for a long while before anyone spoke.

Bowdie finished his bar first, then rolled the wrapper into a small ball and glanced at the old man staring out the window. "Casey," he asked, "is that thing out there really a Time Machine?"

Casey pulled his face away and looked into Bowdie's eyes. "Son, that thing out there is the Devil himself in a mechanical body."

Bowdie glanced at Riley than back, "What do you mean?"

The old man shook his head and made a face that created worry lines around his eyes. "What I mean is that thing out there can change everything."

"Everything," Bowdie asked.

The old man nodded. "Just think about it son. Let's say you and your friend there," he glanced at Riley than back, "just suppose you two had somebody you didn't like, someone you wanted to get rid of and leave no trace. All you'd have to do is throw them in that machine and zap them off to some other time in the past, than bingo, never heard of again.

The old man leaned back in his chair and folded his arms. "Or, what if you were to go back in time and murder famous people while they were still young; murder them before they became famous; like Abraham Lincoln for example. Think about it. Instead of Lincoln being our president during the Civil War, what if someone else had been and the South won. Today we'd be the Divided States of America, and maybe, still have slavery."

Bowdie frowned. "That'd be a pile of cow crap."

Casey nodded, "A pile in deed. And what if someone went back and made sure your parents never met. You wouldn't even be here."

Riley bit at his lip, listening quietly. Finally he joined the conversation. "Casey, I believe Mr. Climers would use that machine just the way you described."

Casey made a worried face and glanced around the room, than in a whisper said. "That's right son, and he's going to."

CHAPTER SEVENTEEN

Casey rose from his chair and walked to the counter. He poured a cup of coffee then returned. When seated he asked, "How well do you boys know your history?" Following a sip he asked a second question before either had time to reply, "You two ever hear of the Spanish explorer, Francisco Vasquez de Coronado?"

Bowdie answered immediately, "Sure, he discovered the Grand Canyon."

Casey nodded. "That's right, but it wasn't the Grand Canyon he was searching for." Casey took another sip. "Coronado had heard the legend of seven wondrous cities made of gold and silver. Supposedly they existed somewhere in what is now the American West. He and his men set out on expedition in 1541, explicitly to find them. He believed them to be the richest cities in the world, and if they were found today, their worth would be in the very high trillions."

"Wow!" Riley said.

"Wow, indeed." Casey told him. "And I've got an even bigger wow for you. They really exist."

"Man, jump into my space," Bowdie said, "They're real and worth trillions?"

"Trillions" Casey nodded.

"Wait a minute." Riley interrupted. "If those cities exist today, especially here in the United States, then why hasn't someone already found them?"

Casey shrugged. "Mostly because no one truly believes they're real and taken the time to seriously search. Besides, they're well hidden, have been for hundreds of years."

"If they're hidden Casey, and have never been found, why do you believe they exist?"

"Because of a map, or half a map I should say, stolen right here in this mansion a hundred and forty some years ago, by Judge Murder himself. According to the story he stole it from a guest staying here with him, a professor Robert Hale who taught History at Purdue."

"How did the judge know he had the map?"

"That, no one knows. But the story goes he found it in one of the professor's trunks."

Immediately Riley recalled the trunk Frog and Harvey had taken from upstairs. "Was it the trunk from the first room on the first floor?"

Casey shrugged than took a sip, "Don't know. What I do know is a little over a year ago Mr. Climers rediscovered the map. This time he found it in a trunk belonging to the judge."

"Wow," Bowdie said, "From trunk to trunk to greedy skunk."

Casey glanced at Bowdie with a nod, than turned back to Riley. "The trunk you're referring to, Mr. Climers believes may have belonged to Professor Hale. According to recently discovered records the Professor stayed in that room. So Mr. Climers had the trunk brought down and torn apart."

"Obviously he was hoping to find the other half of the map, correct?" Riley asked.

"Correct," Casey said, "but the trunk turned out to be full of gold bars and woman's clothes." "Wow," Bowdie said, "Professor Hale was a cross-dresser?"

Casey's forehead wrinkled as he looked at Bowdie, "Well I don't know about that, but whatever the case, we do know the Professor made an enemy out of the Judge. According to the old courthouse records Murda had him hung on June 23, 1888."

"Hung for what", Riley asked.

"Murder," Casey said softly, "but it was probably a drummed-up charge."

Riley bit at his lip. "Okay, let me get this straight. The old Judge stole the map from Professor Hale's trunk, hid it in his trunk where it remained for over a hundred and forty years. And now, Mr. Climers has it." Riley shrugged his shoulders, "But how did Mr. Climer's know the Judge had the map in the first place?"

Casey swallowed the last sip of coffee in his cup. "No idea. It was through means unknown to any of us. I guess when you have money and power you have access to privileged information. All we know is, one by one he covertly approached us and by promise of money or threat, convinced us to come here and work on the project. "

Casey excused himself and left to refill his coffee cup; when back he took a sip as he sat again. "All of us here have at one time or another worked on the Time Travel Task Force, code named: Quantum Odyssey Project. The Secretary of Defense has sanctioned the project top priority, but because of technology limitations progress has been little more than a crawl for over a decade."

Bowdie jumped in, "So what's going on here is a top-secret government project, right?"

Casey shook his head. "No, the government has no idea. Top-Secret yes, but only Mr. Climers and the handpicked crew you see here are aware of what is happening to this day."

Riley sighed. "Casey, I'm missing something. If there has been no progress for ten years, why suddenly is it here built and functional?"

Casey sipped again, "Mr. Climers copied all classified information concerning the Quantum Odyssey Project. He then assembled all of us here; the best in the business if you will. Along with other stolen technologies we worked and reworked, designed, and redesigned again and again until finally… success; if you wish to call it that." Casey frowned as he took another sip of coffee.

Riley ran his hand through his hair. "Okay, so we have a Time Travel-Vehicle and a map showing the location of the Seven Cities of Cibola, worth trillions today. There's a connection here somewhere, right?"

Casey gave a nod. "There is. Remember, Mr. Climers possess only one half of the map; the half telling him the seven cities are located somewhere in the state of Arizona; exactly where we don't know. Arizona is a big state. It would take a millennium of lifetimes to even come close to finding the cities without the other half of the map".

Riley thoughtfully chewed on his lip, "So where is the other half?"

"We don't know." Casey said, "Mr. Climers is counting on Professor Hale to give us that information."

Bowdie glanced quickly at Riley then back to Casey. "How can Professor Hale tell them, he's…?" Bowdie slapped his forehead, "Duh, the Time Machine, right?"

Casey nodded. "That's right son. You see, Mr. Climers is sending someone back to June 22, 1888, the day before the hanging. They will go to the jail, locate Professor Hale and by whatever means necessary, convince him to tell the location of the other half. Once this person has it, they will return and give it to Mr. Climers, who will then use it to locate the Seven Cities and become so rich, he'll make Bill Gates look like a pauper."

Riley understood clearly now; Mr. Climers said he and Bowdie would be going on a trip, to a place where no one living today had ever been. He was sending them back in time to June 22, 1888. And it was a one-way trip.

CHAPTER EIGHTEEN

One of the workers stuck their head in the lounge. "Hey Casey, Mr. Climers wants to see you right away, he's upstairs by the suit of armor." Casey rose from his chair mumbling, "What did I do now?" Grabbing his cup he gulped the remainder of his coffee, than looked at the boys. "You two sit right here. Don't leave this room and I mean it?"

Riley and Bowdie gave a nod, and he was gone. They watched him disappear behind the TT-V. Neither could actually see him, but he went to the brick wall and waited while the door opened. Riley counted the time from opening to closing; exactly twenty-five seconds.

Riley turned to Bowdie. "We have to make a run for it."

Bowdie agreed but his face showed concern. Riley understood. Frog's warning had been strong. It was obvious the big man disliked Bowdie, and given the opportunity would do just as he had promised.

But what else was there to do? In just a short while they would be thrown into the TT-V and hurtled back in time, never to see their families again. If Casey went out through the secret passage door, than he would come back the same way. That meant sooner or later it would be opening again; and that would be their opportunity. It was their one and only chance.

"Are you up to this? You scared?" Riley asked.

Bowdie give a nod. "I'm up to it. Am I scared? Oh yeah. I haven't wet my Fruit of the Looms yet, but if Frog catches me this time I will saturate em." Bowdie took a deep breath, "Look Riley," he said, his face serious, "we have to make a deal."

"What kind of deal?" Riley asked.

"You have to promise that if only one of us makes it, they keep going and get help; no matter what."

For a long while Riley stared into the face of his best friend, considering his words. He knew Bowdie was right, but leaving him behind, if that's how it went down, would not be easy. If caught again, Frog would show no mercy; and even if he did, the Time Machine would be sending him back alone to a time when life was difficult, almost impossible.

He'd be stuck in a period when family and friends were not even born yet. How could a kid from 2023 survive in 1888? Indians were still massacring and taking scalps, there would be no electricity, indoor toilets, or showers. And the horror of horrors- Sam Walton wouldn't even be heard of yet...there would be no Wall-Mart stores.

Not wanting too, Riley agreed and offered his hand, "Okay," he said, "I pray that's not what happens, but that's the deal."

Bowdie took Riley's hand realizing it could be the last time they would ever shake again. It was a troublesome thought. Releasing their grip they turned and stared out through the glass partition silent and sober.

Over the top of the Time Machine they could see a small section of the brick wall. The plan was simple. The moment they saw the door begin to open they'd make a dash for it, out into the basement and up the stairs, through the mansion, out into the yard, then into the woods and out the other side to home. The chances were slim but put simply; it was their only hope.

There was a lot of activity around the Machine. The workers resembled bees buzzing around a hive. Riley wondered how long the final preparations would take: a day, an hour, only minutes.

Pulling his stare from the TT-V he glanced at Bowdie. His friend was staring out through the partition lost in thought. What a friend, Riley thought. No way could he leave him behind. And although Bowdie would never admit it, there was no way he'd leave him behind either. Thick or thin, good or bad, they were in this together.

MURDA MANSION

CHAPTER NINETEEN

Riley let out a deep breath, than it happened! The door began opening. They could see the wall begin its slide inward. Riley looked quickly at Bowdie. "This is it. You ready?"

Bowdie nodded. "Let's do it." Riley opened the glass door and out they charged.

The way was clear and at first it was easy. Twice someone stepped in their path, but they effortlessly maneuvered around them. The door came into view. Through it stepped Casey followed by Harvey. Behind him came Frog. Once inside all three moved clear of the door so it could close. That's when Riley and Bowdie flew past, out into the basement.

Frog turned in time to glimpse the two vanishing into the fading light. "Hey, you flea bags get back here." Bolting through the opening after them he yelled for Harvey to follow.

Behind them the door slid into place and darkness swallowed the basement. Frog and Harvey turned on flashlights.

Riley and Bowdie blinked trying to gain vision within the darkness. Then Bowdie tripped over something, tumbled to the floor, rolled, but was back on his feet in seconds. The beams from Frog and Harvey's flashlights bounced in the blackness. They were gaining ground quickly.

Riley and Bowdie reached the stairs with Frog less than twenty feet behind. Side by side the two clambered up the wooden steps, Adrenalin surging, hearts hammering. The door grew closer. Three steps left, two, one; the door opened suddenly, and their momentum sent them crashing into Mr. Climers. He staggered backward but managed to grab their collars, "Oh no, you don't." He said.

Frog reached the top noticeably out of breath. Bending, he rested his hands on his knees. Then Harvey came bounding up, he too breathing laboriously.

Climers forced a smile. "It would appear you gentlemen have no desire to ride in my shiny little Machine." He shrugged, "I can understand your apprehension. Suppose I offer you both a choice." Bowdie and Riley looked at one another. Climers continued. "The choice is this; return with me to the TT-V for your little scheduled ride, or I turn you over to Frog who will take you for a ride of his own." Either way, you won't be coming back." Climers paused briefly before adding "Personally, I recommend the TT-V. The Time Machine won't hurt nearly as much as what Frog will do to the both of you."

Riley and Bowdie continued to stare at one another. There really was no choice; Frog would kill them for sure. "Well," Climers said growing impatient, "which will it be gentlemen, Frog or Machine?"

"Some choice," Riley said grimly, turning his eyes up to Mr. Climers; "Machine."

"And you Young man?" Climers said to Bowdie.

Bowdie looked up at Climers, paused a moment, then pulled his stare to Frog. The big man had regained his breath and was grinning with evil at Bowdie. "I'm with Riley," Bowdie said holding his stare, "I'd rather be sent back in time forever, than go anywhere with that reptilian looking homo sapien."

Frog's smile vanished. "What did you just call me, you butt- worm?" Frog grabbed for Bowie, but Climers stopped him.

"Not now Frog, you'll have time to play later. Right now we have a deadline. Let's stay focused."

CHAPTER TWENTY

They returned to the TT-V where Riley and Bowie were placed back in the lounge with Casey. The old man poured himself another cup of coffee and sat. several minutes passed before he said anything. When he did he was stern.

"For the life of me what were you thinking? Do you have any idea who you're dealing with?" Casey had asked the questions but again didn't wait for an answer. "Mr. Climers works for the C.I.A., Central Intelligence Agency. He's the top dog and considered a Knight in Shining Armor. Frog and Harvey work directly for him. I don't know about Harvey, but Frog's nickname is Hatchet Man. Want to guess why?"

Casey quit talking then and shook his head. He looked out through the glass partition and stared. There was silence again. Riley placed his elbows on the table and rested his chin in his hands, staring out through the glass himself. He watched the technicians readying the Machine.

He had traveled with his mom and dad to Arizona once. They had driven by Van, and it had taken forever. The distance added up to well over two-thousand miles one-way; a very long, boring haul. Riley sighed; but he'd gladly do it again in a heart-beat compared to the trip coming up: two-thousand miles wasn't nearly as far as a hundred and forty years into the past.

Sadness welled up inside him. He loved his family and did not want to leave. He had a good life at home. His parents were the best. The idea of leaving them…forever; was something he couldn't imagine.

Casey took a sip of coffee, than set his cup down. "Look boys," he said. They turned to look at him. Casey's voice was low; so low they strained to hear him, "I shouldn't be telling you this, and if they found out they'd kill me. But I've got to say it." Riley and Bowdie looked at one another, a strange new hope arising in their hearts. Casey laced his fingers and rested his hands on the table in front of him. "There's a way back."

"How?" they asked eagerly.

"When the Machine lands, or stops, I should say, stay with it. It will be returning in 24 hours from that exact moment." Casey glanced out through the glass again nervously, his face covered with worry lines. "But there's a catch," he added, bringing his eyes back to the boys, "the man they are sending back with you is, Frog."

Bowdie rolled his eyes, "Freaking figures."

"If," Casey went on, "a problem develops and Frog has to stay, the plan is that he will have one month. The Machine will once again return on the evening of July 22 at exactly 7:30. If he or you miss that ride, there will be no other."

Riley asked hurriedly. "You said if there were no problems. What kind of problems might there be, Casey?"

"The map. In the event Frog must track it down, it will allow him time to do so."

Frog and Harvey came in and Casey fell silent. Frog had changed clothes. He was now dressed in a swallowtail black suit resembling a tuxedo. He was also wearing a tall black hat like honest Abe; but it certainly didn't fit his personality. On his feet were brown shoes with white tops. Obviously they were clothes worn by men living in 1888. The idea no doubt was to ensure he blended in.

Frog folded his arms and let a sinister grin show on his chubby face. In his frog like voice he told them, "Well it's time for our trip. And just for your information, when we get to where we're going there will be no Mr. Climers to keep me from doing what I want." He looked directly at Bowdie, "You, you smart mouthed little sneak, I have something special planned for you."

Frog unfolded his arms and pulled a cigar stub from his coat pocket. Sticking it between his lips he said, "Now come on you multi-colored trash maggots, it's time for the ride of your life."

CHAPTER TWENTY-ONE

With reluctance Riley and Bowie followed Frog out of the Lounge where they found Mr. Climers waiting beside the open door of the TT-V.

The nicely dressed boss folded his arms smiling, "Gentlemen, the time is here. You're about to take that trip I promised, travel back to a time when the telephone is just coming into use. There will be no central heat or air, no refrigerators or microwaves, and much to your shocking terror, you'll find Television, DVDs and Dolby-Surround-Sound have not yet even been thought of," he shrugged, "gee, now that I think about it, you won't even have radio.

Climers unfolded his arms and brought his hands together as if he were about to pray. He touched his fingers to his lips. "I suppose I could go on forever about the changes that await you, but I haven't the time. So just let me finish by saying, best of luck and have a prosperous pre-life... or would that be after-life?"

Climers winked, then turned to walk away but stopped. Looking back over his shoulder, he added, "Just think gentlemen, if you take good care of yourselves, and live another hundred and forty plus years, give or take, you can go back home and see your mommy and daddy again. His head lifted and he roared with laughter while turning to walk away again.

It was a cruel laugh, one that brought home the realization of what was about to happen. Riley looked at Bowdie. And when Bowdie saw the fear in Riley's eyes it angered him. Bowdie shouted after Climers, "Hey Mr. Climers." Once again Climers stopped and looked back over his shoulder. When he did, Bowdie gave him the finger. And this time Riley didn't stop him.

Climers looked at Frog. "When you get there, I want that smart-mouthed kid turned into roadkill." Frog smiled for Bowdie, "My pleasure boss."

CHAPTER TWENTY-TWO

So this was it Riley thought. Game over! Going home was only something they could dream about now. No more mom and dad, no more family, no more anything from 2023. Riley wondered what his dad would do if he were in this situation. Actually he knew. His Dad would hold up his head, keep his cool, he'd be positive, get a grip, tell himself there was a way out, there is always a way out.

Riley looked at the door of the TT-V. it stood open like the mouth of a starved, crazed monster, waiting to swallow them and send their digested remains to a world of doom. Riley whispered under his breath… "1888."

He had a frightful thought. What if, after he's there, the need to see a dentist arises? In those days there were no medications like Novocain, for numbing. If they pulled a tooth back then, they simply grabbed a pair of pliers and held you down in the chair ignoring your screams. Riley shuddered; and what about Doctors? What if he had to have his tonsils removed or an appendectomy? It was a known fact; old-time hospitals weren't very sanitary. Thousands died from infection.

Frog suddenly grabbed Riley by the collar and belt and physically stuffed him through the small doorway of the Machine; Bowdie was shoved in right behind him. Then Frog himself wiggled in.

There were only two seats, so Frog forced Riley and Bowdie into one, side by side, then snapped the seat-belt into place. Plopping into the other he snapped in himself. Eyes wide, the boys looked over the TT-V 's interior. The walls were padded with thick, blue quilting. It reminded them of a padded room inside an insane asylum. There were no windows and the interior was small, barely room to accommodate the two seats.

Climers stuck his head through the opening, "Everything is set, Frog," he said, "you know what to do, correct?" Frog replied with a nod that showed irritation. It was obvious he hated taking orders. "Now remember," Climers added, "you are only to extract the information and retrieve the item, nothing else. He must hang just as history dictates. Is that clear?"

Again Frog nodded, irritably. "Yes, Mr. Climers, that is clear."

Climers smiled briefly, but it was only for show. "Fine." he said "Now remember, if you must search for the item, you have only a short time to find it, or you know what happens."

Silently Frog gave another aggravated nod, this time offering no verbal reply. Climers glanced over at the boys to insure they had no idea what he was talking about. Little do you know, Riley thought.

Climers removed his head and the door closed. Resembling a watertight hatch found on naval warships, the little round wheel in the center of the door spun and locked. They were sealed in.

Riley and Bowdie's hearts were pounding. Panic heightened. They were trapped like mice in a cage; two mice and a big Rat. There was a small round site-glass at the top of the iron door, and it was the only thing connecting them to the outside world.

Riley glanced at Bowdie knowing exactly what his best friend was thinking. *Here they were, locked helplessly inside a Time-Travel Vehicle ready to send them back in time a hundred and forty years, with a madman who planned to do bodily harm to the both of them the moment they arrived. A sigh slipped from Riley's lips. Things couldn't possibly get any worse.*

Then Frog grinned. "You little girls aren't scared, are you?" Neither of them replied. Speaking with the cigar tight between his teeth, Frog told them, "It hurts. It's worse than any roller coaster ride you've ever been on; lots of pain, with a heartbeat that's wild and erratic. Your body will sweat, and your skin will turn red first, then white as a sheet. You'll want to scream, but you can't because of the centrifugal force. You maggots have any idea what centrifugal force is? It's when you're traveling at a speed so fast, you can't move, even if your life depends on it. The force holds you frozen in your seat until one of two things happen…the machine finally comes to a stop, or the speed just keeps increasing until you explode like a human bomb; blood, guts and brains splattered all over the place." Bowdie and Riley made a face.

Frog burst into laughter, a mental-illness kind of laugh that showed his true dark side, a laugh edged with the cruelty that filled his mind and flowed through his body like a deadly poison.

Someone tapped on the little window then and gave a thumbs-up. Frog nodded and leaned back in his seat. Still clenching the cigar between his teeth he winked at the boys. "This is it you brainless balls of snot. 1888 here we come."

CHAPTER TWENTY-THREE

There was a scant movement of the Machine, a slight jar. Riley bit nervously at his lip. Five more seconds passed, and the Machine began to spin slowly in a counter-clockwise circle. So far, Riley thought, it was like the start of a ride at Disney World…not too bad.

Quickly Frog reached up and pulled the cigar from his mouth, sticking it back in his pocket. The Machine began picking up speed and the boys gripped the edge of their seat. They were spinning faster and faster.

Within twenty seconds the force was such that it was impossible to move without great effort. Frog closed his eyes. Sweat was forming on his brow. It was clear to Riley why the seat- belts were there. Without them, they would have been thrown from their seats prior to the centrifugal force taking hold.

It had been less than a minute and already the speed was incredible, spinning round and round, growing unbearable. The Machine shook frantically, like a spinning dryer out of balance clanging and banging wildly.

Pressed hard against their seats, they were frozen just as Frog had said. It was a powerful force. Riley tried to lift his arm but couldn't. Incredible pressure pushed hard against their bodies, as if its very intention was to crush them. It was growing impossible to breath; feeling as though their chests could not expand. Heat was increasing inside the Machine. The skin on their face had twisted into a horrible, distorted mass of flesh, pulled and pushed and stretched. Their bodies shook almost uncontrollably, as if their brains were heating to a dangerous level, sending them to the edge of convulsions. The TT-V's shaking grew violent, so fierce they feared it might explode.

Around and around it spun, each rotation taking but a fraction of a second. They were destructive revolutions, whose killing speed promised eventual death to their frail human bodies if it didn't end soon.

Their heads grew light, their minds a distant blur nearing the point of unconsciousness. But Riley fought hard to stay awake. His body wanted to let go, to fall into the world of deep sleep, to stay there until the terrible pain was over; how could any human-being survive this?

Then there came a new level of pain. A stabbing sensation, an agonizing piercing that felt as though someone were thrusting the blade of a sharp knife deep into their chest. Riley tried to scream but nothing came out. He couldn't move his head to see, but he worried for Bowdie. Was he experiencing the same things, or had he gone unconscious?

Riley's heart was slamming inside his chest, a frantic irregular rhythm, a pounding he could feel down to his toes. Was it a sign his heart was ready to stop? Frog had said the heart beat would be affected.

Pain, agony, hurting, the want to go unconscious, Bowdie, mom, dad, pass out, throw-up…these were the things filtering through Riley's thoughts at rapid speed. He struggled to not think about the spinning, for it greatly magnified the feeling of nausea and light hardheadedness. It was useless, however, for his thoughts always returned to it.

What could this trip in the TT-V be compared too: a wild carnival ride, a racing car, a fighter jet traveling at the speed of sound, the crushing velocity of the space shuttle? Wait, he knew… the inside of a giant blender. "Stop it Riley" He screamed at himself.

The inside of the Machine had grown unbearably hot. Droplets of condensation clung to the quilted walls. Riley felt like he was burning up with fever and his clothes were drenched in sweat. Endlessly the Machine whirled in never ending revolutions. How long had it been, minutes or hours? His breathing had dangerously slowed, and the pain in his chest grew worse.

Like it or not, he knew unconsciousness was coming. It was already there waiting. With effort Riley wet his dry lips. Here they were he thought, traveling back through time. Now more than ever he wished he were his dad. He would know how to survive in 1888. He and Bowdie were in no way ready for this. What did two young boys from the year 2023, know about being on their own and staying alive in a time so long ago?

Riley felt himself begin to pass out. "NO" he screamed in his head. But it felt so good, it was something he wanted, needed. His chin dropped to his chest. It was comfortable, a wonderful feeling, like crawling into a nice warm bed.

Then the realization hit. "WAIT! Your head, it's hanging down, the centrifugal force, it's letting up!" With effort, very slowly, Riley lifted his chin. He remained dizzy and felt sick to his stomach, feeling the urge to throw-up, but he fought it. His head spun around and around, his eyes remained blurry, everything seemed a blend of colors with no shape or form. But his breathing was returning to normal, and his heart was quieting.

Several minutes passed before his eyes returned to normal vision. When they did he took a deep breath and sighed. The inside of the TT-V lay draped in soft, orange light. He could make out the medal door and its small glass window.

Outside, red and blue lights were flashing. His thinking was clearing, his strength returning, and the dizziness was nearly gone. And most importantly, he was alive! He was breathing! He was here... or was he? Could it be really June 22, 1888?

CHAPTER TWENTY-FOUR

All of Riley's sense had returned to normal. Then he remembered… BOWDIE! His best friend sat slumped in the seat, not moving. It was panic. Riley shook him wildly; Bowdie stirred and moaned, and just as Riley sighed with relief Bowdie looked up blinked wildly.

Little by little his eyes focused. Following in a deep breath he told Riley. "Man that was some ride. I feel like we've just rode Mission Space at Disney World forty-nine times in a row."

"More like fifty." Riley said.

"No way," Bowdie told him, "it was definitely forty-nine. Fifty would have killed us."

"Yeah," Riley agreed, "I came an inch from hurling."

"Me too," Bowdie said turning to look at Frog. The fat man sat slumped and unconscious in his seat. "And if I had tossed my cookies," Bowdie said, "I'd have pointed my projectile puke assortment straight in his direction." Bowdie paused a moment continuing to stare at the fat man, "Do you think he's dead?"

Riley made a face, "I don't know."

Frog's head hung down and his arms dangled at his side. The seatbelt was holding him in place; Riley disconnected their own and they stood. Riley knew they would have to check Frog's pulse to know for sure if he were dead or alive. And like it or not, the only way to do it was to touch him.

The pulse would be on the side of the neck. He had learned that in CPR class, it was called the Carotid Artery. Riley's hand reached out, stretching toward the pudgy throat.

This was another one of those things Riley hated to do. They were standing less than a foot from the man who had been ordered to turn Bowdie into roadkill.

He touched his skin and pressed. The very feel of him made Riley shiver. He could detect no pulse and pulled quickly away. Relief washed over him. From behind, Bowdie spoke in a whisper. "Is he dead?"

Riley nodded. "Yeah, he has to be, there's no pulse."

Both felt spooked standing in tight quarter with a dead body, yet they sighed together in harmony. Turning, they moved to the medal door and glanced through the little round window. Beyond it there was darkness, with the exception of the soft blue and red lights flashing around the Machine.

Gripping the round wheel Riley began spinning it. It whirled rapidly and in seconds made a clicking sound and stopped. The door jarred open. Riley gave it a shove and it swung outward coming to rest against the Machine.

Instantly the string of red and blue lights stopped flashing and everything went dark. Somewhere inside the Machine they heard a humming sound, and the colored lights came back on, this time shining steadily. Beyond the Machine door darkness lay like thick shadows.

In silence they stared, questions racing through their minds: where were they, where had they landed, what should they do now, where would they go, and most important, who or what was out there?

CHAPTER TWENTY-FIVE

Thankfully the red and blue lights helped to illuminate the area. Little at a time their eyes were adjusting. Bowdie leaned out of the doorway. "Riley" he said with excitement, "I see a brick wall with a doorway directly in front of us. "Take a look!"

Riley leaned over Bowdie's shoulder and squinted, "Yeah. I see it."

The red and blue lights seemed to be lighting the area around them with dim, but good visibility. Riley caught his breath. "Bowdie, you know what?"

"What?"

"We know that brick wall. It's the same one we walked through just a few minutes ago; I mean over a hundred and twenty years ago. The only difference is it doesn't have a secret door anymore, it's a regular opening into the other part of the basement."

Bowdie glanced quickly at Riley than back at the wall. "It sure to heck is. We never left Judge Murda's basement."

"Right," Riley said looking at him nervously, "we're still here all right. The only difference is it's now 1888. Do you realize we're not born yet?"

The thought silenced them. Both stood at the Machine's door staring out, wondering the same thing; what now?

Behind them Frog's body remained slumped and motionless. It sounded cold and heartless, but they were relieved he was gone. To the front there was darkness. Above would be the mansion, MURDA MANSION. And in it would be the Judge himself, the Old Neck Stretcher…the man who loved hanging people. And this time he was alive! Riley wondered if he hung young teenagers.

Continuing to stare into the colored darkness, Bowdie finally asked the question neither wanted to face. "Okay, what now?"

Riley shrugged. "I don't know! Casey said the Machine would automatically return in 24 hours. If we're here when it leaves, we'll just go back with it, right?"

Bowdie looked at him. "That's true. But remember, when it gets there Mr. Climers and the others will be waiting, and they'll just send us right back again."

Riley nodded his agreement. "You're right. But I think I have an idea."

"Cool Beans. What?" Bowdie asked.

Riley bit at his lip. "Well, if we were to return with the rest of the map we could use it as a trade. Give it to Mr. Climers in exchange for letting us go."

Bowdie frowned. "Get a brain, Riley. You know what he would do. He'd keep the map and still send us back. It's for sure he can't be trusted."

"That's true. But what if we memorized the map then destroyed it. He would have no choice but let us go in exchange for the information. We'd be the only ones in the world who'd know where the Seven Cities of Cibola are located." Riley paused briefly, "and he'd have to take us with him to show him where they're located. That means a chance to escape."

Bowdie looked back out into the basement considering Riley's idea. He was thinking how much he wished he were an adult. Making decisions always seemed so easy for them. He turned back to Riley.

"Okay." He said. "Let's review your plan. Your suggesting we march straight to the jail and tell Professor Hale he has to give us the map, a map worth billions of dollars. To just hand it over to us, two strange boys claiming they are from the year 2023, sent back in time in a Machine called a TT-V, with a killer who looks and talks like a human Frog." Bowdie gave a nod. "It's slick, Riley. And while we're at it, we'll also tell him we're Wells Fargo agents undercover. Man, he'll be begging us to take the map." Bowdie raised a finger, adding, "But, just in case your plan should fail, we'll fall back on the one I've come up with."

"Great," Riley said, "what?"

"We return with the machine back to Mr. Climers, drop to our freaking knees and plead like beggars for our lives." Shaking his head Bowdie turned back to stare out into the basement.

Riley made a face. *Yeah, the plan did sound a bit ridiculous.*

The red and blue lights continued to shine, lighting the area around the TT-V. The basement was quiet, no sound and no movement; it was as though the world had stopped. Then Bowdie looked once again at Riley. "You know," he said, "My plan sucks, and I'm so crapping scared I'll try anything. Let's give your plan a whirl."

Riley smiled. Just when he was down and out more than he'd ever been in his life, Bowdie was there with a boost of encouragement. No doubt about it, if you had to be sent back in time with someone, Bowdie Pager was the one to be with. He was scared but cool as a fresh D.Q. Chocolate Milkshake.

CHAPTER TWENTY-SIX

Neither wanted to touch the dead body again, so they left Frog in his seat, agreeing to drag him out when they got back. It was procrastination but touching him was an absolute last resort.

Their eyes had fully adjusted to the colored lighting, and they could see quite well now. Riley glanced at his watch, 10:16 a.m. They had about twenty-three and a half hours before the TT-V returned; plenty of time to visit the professor and get back.

The basement looked much like it did when they ran from Frog and Harvey well over a century ago. Crossing through the junk-filled rooms they reached the same stairway they had run up while trying to escape; only now it looked new and felt strong. As he climbed Riley thought about the things Bowdie had said.

First of all, would Professor Hale tell a couple of boys he didn't know where a treasure map worth billions was hidden? Not likely. Secondly, the Professor would be in jail waiting for tomorrows hanging. Could they even get inside to talk with him? And equal to both of those was the question of where was Murda? Was he in the house above somewhere; or in town working, was someone else in the house, family or servants maybe? And what about the other half of the map, where was it? What if it was located far away? Some place they wouldn't have time to reach and get back.

Suddenly they were at the top of the stairs. The two glanced at one another. On the other side of the door would be the kitchen. Both listened but heard no sound. Bowdie turned the knob slowly, then eased the door open, just wide enough for a peak. Seeing no one he motioned for Riley to follow behind.

Crossing through the Kitchen Riley placed a hand on Bowdie's shoulder and whispered, "Maybe we should check Professor Hale's room first. The map might be hidden in it somewhere."

Bowdie whispered back, "That's a fantastic idea. Do you know which room is his?"

"Yes, it's upstairs, first floor first room."

"Good. You take the lead and I'll be right behind you."

Riley frowned as his best friend hurried around him.

The kitchen ended and they entered into the hallway leading to the room with the huge wall mirror. It was there they'd find the stairway. The hallway was long, and their nerves remained on edge. A not-so-pleasant thought crossed Riley's mind; if Judge Murda were to catch them snooping, would he have them arrested and then hung for trespassing? Riley pictured himself hanging at the end of a rope, hands tied behind his back and a black back bag over his head. He saw himself kicking and gasping, his eyes bulging, face turning red, tongue swelling and …Riley bit down hard on his lip. *Knock it off.*

They reached the hallway's end and stopped. On the far side of the room was the mirror. And unlike that stormy night, it was fully in tact with no cracks, and none of the wood trim hung down. The glass glistened, revealing their reflection.

To the left of the mirror was the doorway through which he had seen the shadow that night. And there beside it stood the Suit of Armor; no longer old and tarnished from decades of neglect; now it shined like the purest of silver. Sunlight from the windows caused it to shimmer brightly.

Admiring its awesome sense of power, Riley thought of Camelot and the knights of the roundtable with King Arthur and Sir Lancelot.

How exciting it must have been living in those times, fighting for honor with swords and lances and shields, and riding colorfully draped horses in jousting competitions.

Raising an eyebrow he imagined the Castle of Camelot his home, and within its walls a dazzling decorated chamber of stone. And there in the center of that chamber sat the 'roundtable' surrounded with the King's most trusted knights, each rising their glass in toast, "Hail to King Riley, Hail to Queen Aguilera, Hail to Sir Bowdie, and Hail to Lady Michaela.

"Earth to Riley" Bowdie was shaking his shoulder. "Are we going upstairs or what?"

Riley chased away the day dream. "Yeah, first floor, first door."

The stairway was to their right. The once dust covered carpeting was now soft and vibrant with color. The walls were without holes and every picture hung straight. There was no torn wallpaper and no cockroaches. Riley remarked to Bowdie, "Look at that, not one single cockroach."

Bowdie glanced up the wall, "Yeah, they must have all gotten married."

Riley looked at him, "Bowdie Pager, you're not just brain- lame...you are brain dead!

CHAPTER TWENTY-SEVEN

Upon reaching Hale's room they took one last look around: still no sign of anyone. Slipping through the door they closed it quietly. With the exception of being clean and neat, it all looked the same. Even the trunk sat in its proper place.

Immediately they began a search checking everywhere. They looked in the closet, under the bed, beneath the mattress, behind furniture, rummaged through drawers, and removed everything from the trunk. But they found nothing. Riley glanced at Bowdie with disappointment, "Looks like we go talk to the Professor." Saying nothing, Bowdie nodded.

Riley had barely opened the door to leave when he closed it quickly. Someone was bounding up the stairs. Dodging back into the room they dove for the floor and rolled beneath the bed. Hopefully whoever it was, they weren't coming to Professor Hale's room, but Riley considered the way his luck had been running; sure enough it hadn't changed.

Someone came in and paused just inside the doorway, then moved to the trunk. Kneeling, they opened it and began throwing out its contents. Obviously they were searching for something. What that something was took no guessing. When empty, the person paused, pulled something from their pocket and suddenly there arose a ripping sound. The person was cutting out the trunk's lining.

Riley made a face, why didn't they think of that. But it turned out okay; the searcher didn't find what they were looking for. In anger they flipped over the trunk and stood, than kicked it. Whoever it was, they now paused looking over the room.

To the boys it seemed an eternity. Their hearts pounded, fearing the person might begin searching the rest of the room, including beneath the bed. But that didn't happen; instead, they turned abruptly and stormed out.

Riley and Bowdie lay under the bed for several seconds before daring to move. When they did, they wiggled free and hurried to the doorway. No one was around so they moved to the railing and crouched. Below, a man was exciting through the doorway beside the Suit of Armor. He vanished in seconds, but they had gotten a clear look. Glancing at one another Bowdie said what both were thinking, *what the freaking crap!* He yelled at Riley in a whisper, "I thought you said he was dead!"

Riley shrugged, "He was! At least I thought he was. I guess I didn't check good enough."

"GOOD ENOUGH!" Bowdie exclaimed, "In case you've forgotten, he's the man ordered to turn me into roadkill." Bowdie couldn't stop ranting, "Man, I got to tell you Riley, you may be my best friend, but used toilet paper could check a pulse better than you. The guy's a professional…"

Bowdie never finished his statement. Riley clamped a hand over his mouth, "Get a grip Nit-picker." He said, "We have a bigger problem. Look down there!"

CHAPTER TWENTY-EIGHT

With Riley's hand still clamped over his mouth, Bowdie shifted his eyes glancing down between the railings. A man was standing there staring up. His arms were folded across his chest and the expression on his face told of his displeasure. A solid head of gray hair added distinction to the long black robe he was wearing. There would be no need for introductions. The man looking up was Judge Murda.

Saying nothing, Murda unfolded his arms and wiggled a finger, motioning for them to come down. Although never uttering a word there was authority in the gesture. The two didn't move, yet both were thinking the same thing…We have to run! But the old Judge spoke before their brain put the thought into motion; his voice was deep, and iron handed. "Don't even think about running from me. You hooligans get your tails down hear this minute."

Riley released his hand from Bowdie's mouth, and they rose slowly to their feet. Should we run or not run? The question raged in their heads and the decision had to be made fast. They wanted too. But where would they go? They were trapped; cornered upstairs in the old neck stretcher's house by the man himself.

The Judge raised his voice. "Get down here, now!"

With great reluctance they turned in the direction of the stairway. Bowdie was in front but moved quickly behind Riley.

"Brave man," Riley whispered as Bowdie slipped past, "you had the lead, why didn't you stay there?"

"Respect," Bowdie said, "you're older,"

"OLDER! By three months!" Riley exclaimed.

"Hey, older is older."

Murda yelled, "DO NOT MAKE ME SAY IT AGAIN." This time his voice echoed throughout the house.

Biting his lip, Riley hesitated, but Bowdie nudged him. "Go!"

Slowly, practically huddled, the two moved to the stairway leading down. Again they weren't saying a word but wondering the same thing- *would the old Judge hang a couple of young innocent boys?* One at a time they took each step, no particular hurry. When they finally reached the bottom the old neck stretcher was there waiting.

Although taller, the Judge was really a short man. He was noticeably over weight, but well groomed. His hair was neat, his face close shaven, and his cologne or whatever they used in 1888, smelled of Lilacs.

Murda carried a wooden cane and leaned on it with both hands as he spoke. "Now," he asked in a voice radiating authority, "suppose you two ragamuffins explain to me just what it is you're doing in my house."

Riley and Bowdie exchanged glances, waiting for the other to think of something. Neither could think of anything. Murda grew impatient. "WELL?"

Seconds passed before Bowdie stuck his hands in his pockets and cleared his throat. He looked quickly at Riley than to Judge Murda, "Sir, we're Wells Fargo agents."

Murda frowned, "I don't think so."

Bowdie swallowed. "Would you believe Pinkerton Men?"

"NO! Now I want the God's honest truth out of you."

"Okay," Bowdie said. "Here it is. We just arrived from

another time… zone. We're here to see Professor Hale. We heard he is staying here with you."

Raising his eyebrows Murda asked, "And what might be your business with him?"

Bowdie was suddenly stumped, and Riley jumped in. "We're hoping to enroll in College."

Murda moved his eyes to Riley. "College, and just how old are you two?"

"Sixteen" Riley lied.

The Judge made a funny face. "You look awfully small to be that old."

Bowdie cut in "Yes sir, we do…we are. But you see our great grandparents were dwarfs.

Murda frowned. "You two are brothers than?"

In the same instant Riley blurted out yes and Bowdie blurted out no. They looked angrily at one another and Murda spoke again. "Well, which is it? I'd say the difference in your color seems to lean toward the answer being no."

"You see," Bowdie added quickly, "Both our moms and dads worked for a circus in New York. But they didn't want us to have to live like that: twenty-hour days, mean bosses, poor nutrition, no medical coverage, low minimum wage…that's why we're here. They wanted us to have a better life. "Yeah," Riley chimed in, "our goals are to become Lawyers, and someday, a Judge, just like you."

Murda seemed to warm up then. "Well. That certainly is a worthwhile endeavor. However, I'm afraid talking to Professor Hale will do you no good. He's in jail, waiting to be hung tomorrow."

"Wow." Bowdie exclaimed with phony surprise. "What did he do?"

Judge Murda's expression changed. "I think it's time you two got on your way. My suggestion is to go to the college and talk with someone else. I'm heading into town, and I'll give you a ride to the Bridge. You can cross the river and walk to the campus from there."

Both feared the idea of having to ride with the old Judge, but the last thing they wanted was to make him angry. So pretending to be thankful, they accepted his hospitality with near fake looking smiles.

CHAPTER TWENTY-NINE

They left the mansion riding in an open carriage. Drawn by a single horse, it was reined by a man dressed in a black suit and tall hat like the one Frog wore. As the carriage rolled along Riley looked things over.

The woods dividing Murda Mansion and the area where his mom and dad's house would one day sit; looked close to the same, except for the well-traveled buggy-road they were now taking. In Riley's time the road was grown over and remained only a narrow foot path.

Suddenly they burst into the clearing where his housing project stood…or at least would. It was shocking. Instead of the track of beautiful, two-story homes; it was now open fields with grazing cows and horses. Riley realized more than ever, just how very alone in this strange world he and Bowdie were.

Murda pulled a cigar from his coat pocket and lit it using a wooden match he struck against his boot sole. When lit, he asked, "So tell me, what is it they call you boys? Got names?"

Bowdie blurted it out, "Sure do, Got Milk?"

Murda frowned. "What?"

Bowdie was smiling but lost it. "Sorry. "I'm Bowdie Pager and this is Riley McCaden."

The Judge looked at Riley. "How do you spell your last name, son?" Riley spelled it and the Judge raised his eyebrows. "It's for sure spelled the same. Are you any relation to Daniel McCaden, the Druggist on main?"

Riley stared long into the Judge's eyes without realizing what he was doing. In his head a mixture of emotions had suddenly exploded: surprise, hope, anxiety, excitement, and stupidity. The Judge's question changed everything concerning their situation.

Although Riley had found no personal interest in it, his dad was an avid researcher of the McCaden family tree. Daniel McCaden was indeed his relation; the man was his great, great Grandfather.

In his dad's collection of old photos there had been two of Daniel: one with his wife and children, and the other of only him and his wife; what was her name…Mary, Margaret, Mel, Marilyn? Whatever it was, Riley thought, he had seen the photos years ago, when he was only seven. And, he nodded to himself, he knew exactly where Daniel and…what the heck was her name? As if switching on a light it popped suddenly into his head…MARIE!

Riley knew exactly where Daniel and Marie McCaden lived; on South Street, just up the hill a few blocks from down town; in the very house his grandmother still lives in 2023. He knew the house well for he had spent countless weekends there with her while growing up.

Judge Murda reached out with his boot toe and tapped Riley's leg. "Hey boy, I'm talking to you."

Startled, Riley gave the Judge a puzzled look than realized he had been lost in thought. "Sorry," he apologized. "Yes sir, I am related to Daniel McCaden," he told him, "In fact, we're going to pay him a visit as soon as we're finished at the college."

Murda took another puff from his cigar, lifted his face and blew a smoke ring. Riley was relieved the Judge had not asked how they were related. That would have been difficult to explain.

The carriage took them down Main Street toward the bridge. To Riley and Bowdie, it was a trip through the Twilight Zone. They were riding through the same Lafayette they had left little more an hour ago, yet it was different. Most of the streets were dirt, although a few such as main were laid with brick.

Other horse and buggies and single riders passed them constantly, with the hoofs of the horses clicking as they pranced. The animals whinnied a lot and often raised their tails to dump a pile right there in the streets as they walked.

Many of the men were dressed in suits similar to the one Frog wore, and ladies wearing long colorful dresses with wide brimmed hats strolled the sidewalks chatting and gazing in storefront windows. Store owners were out front sweeping walkways or stacking goods for display, always smiling and greeting those passing by.

Many of the buildings, even the courthouse, were recognizable yet different somehow. Although it was all a bit exciting, it brought home the stark realization they were definitely a very long way from home.

In the four hundred block of downtown they passed a store front with a large picture-widow. Judge Murda gestured with the hand holding the cigar. "That's McCaden' s place."

Riley turned quickly to get a look inside. It was dark but he caught a glimpse of someone moving around. Above the door hung a sign that read:

McCaden Drug & Mercantile

406 MAIN.

As the buggy rolled past Riley remained twisted in his seat staring. He wanted to leap from the buggy and run charging into the store. To explain the terrible fix he and Bowdie were in, to ask for help; to plead. Surely his great, great grandfather would listen…than again maybe not.

Yes, Daniel McCaden was family; but he and Bowdie were one hundred and forty years from the future. Convincing anyone of that would prove near to impossible.

CHAPTER THIRTY

The McCaden store was well out of sight by the time they reached the Bridge. The driver halted the horse and set the brake. Hurriedly Riley and Bowdie climbed out as Murda took a puff from his cigar, "Now don't you boys get into any trouble, it'd pain me to have to hang a couple of future lawyers."

Releasing the brake, the driver shook the reins and made a clicking sound. The buggy lurched forward and rolled away with horse hoofs clopping against the bricks. Riley and Bowdie stood watching until the buggy rounded a corner.

Turning, they stared at the bridge stretching across the Wabash River. Bowdie told Riley, "Man, we are in another dimension." The big wooden structure before them was a long covered one, wide enough maybe to allow a Horse and Buggy like Judge Murda's to pass one another. To the right of the bridge below, three Steamboats were tied to a long wooden dock. Two rocked gently from the slow flowing river and the other was being unloaded by a long line of men.

Bowdie recognized a building, although longer here, in 2023 it was Sargent Prestins Barr and grill. And to the left of the bridge came another shock. A giant wooden building complex with pens holding pigs all around it stood two stories high. Between the complex and row of other businesses and homes sat what was the Erie Canal. Two horse drawn boats were being pulled along. Both boys were spellbound.

Across the river where the Wabash Landing use to be, or would be someday, there were a few scattered houses with fields and crops growing; no Movie Theater, no Hotels, no Restaurants, no Starbucks, Gas-Station, Parking Garage, Reilley's Plaza with Train Depot; no nothing, just no nothing. And freaky was the hill down the way going up to Purdue University, State Street. It was gravel with each side lined with mostly rundown housed surrounded with trees and brush and weeds. And dear God, there was no McDonalds or historical Triple X; that history hadn't even become history yet!. And beyond all this, nothing; there was NO Chauncey Hill with college students everywhere wearing out the pavement, walking and crossing and talking and jogging. All was gone, no high-rise housing, nothing but woods a few more scattering of small rundown houses.

Riley and Bowdie stopped their shock-looking and glanced at one another. Ignoring the pounding of their hearts and fighting back tears, they stared at one another in silence. The world they had known all their life was gone. Going back in time, Riley thought, seemed exciting when you were watching it happen in a movie eating popcorn and sitting in a soft comfortable seat. This however, was not; there was no excitement here, only a struggle to control the slow, steady rise of panic and despair.

Fighting their despair, they turned looking back into the city. Down there they took in many of the buildings they recognized and many they didn't. Most streets were not yet bricked, and none paved, most dirt. And from history class in school both recognized the rail road tracks running through 5th street, but in their time of 2023, they were covered over with blacktop and not visible. There were other rail tracks they could see throughout the city of Lafayette, 1888. But, again because of history in school, they both knew these were rails for the new Electrified Street Car System ready to be put in use this very year in Indiana History. And while it really didn't help, they kind of felt special, standing here now, looking at the tracks knowing they were witnessing and be one of the Lafayette citizens who could say they walked on and saw the new laid tracks of 1888. Somehow that made them feel better.

Riley looked at Bowdie, "Well, what say we mosey on down to see my great great Granddad! Bowdie smiled with a high-five. Riley replied and they walked on down into the 1888 city of Lafayette, Indiana.

Riley's mind was racing. At 406 Main he'd find family. But again he wondered; could he convince Daniel McCaden of what was happening?

A long wagon pulled by two horses rattled past. Stacked with loose hay it was driven by a young man wearing worn jeans and shirt, badly scuffed boots and wide brimmed gray hat. The driver nodded then rolled onto the covered bridge.

Riley and Bowdie watched until the wagon was well inside and crossing the Wabash River, then continued their walk to the only hope they had in this new strange world.

Both wondered, and greatly worried about the initial contact. Riley knew the odds were huge that his great, great grandfather would only laugh when they told him. But he was their big hope. Their only hope. They had to try.

CHAPTER THIRTY-ONE

When they arrived at the Drug Store the place still looked dark inside. Riley pressed his nose to the window peering in. Far in the back he could see a dim light and occasionally catch a glimpse of someone moving about. "Come on," he told Bowdie, "let's see if there's a back door."

They cut through an alley and found what they were looking for. Following one long nervous glance at Bowdie, Riley bit at his lip and knocked. The door rattled noisily. They heard mumbling inside and the sound of someone approaching. Then it opened.

Riley caught his breath. Great, great grandfather looked just like the old-time picture his father had in his collection. He was wearing a short, well-groomed beard and loose red hair fell nearly to the top of his shoulders. A pair of green McCaden eyes stared out form a jovial, happy face. His dad's old photo had been in black and white, but the color of the eyes and hair came as no surprise; after all, Daniel McCaden was Irish.

"Mornin' to ya' lads, what can I be doin' fer ya'?"

An Irish accent too Riley thought. For some reason he wasn't expecting that and it took him by surprise. But it was cool. Riley remembered Daniel had been the first McCaden to come to America to start a new life. Nervously Riley bit at his lip not sure where to start, so he began with a question.

"Are you Daniel McCaden?"

"I, tis me in the flesh, lad."

Riley stammered on. "Sir, you don't know who I am, but we're related. My name is Riley McCaden."

Daniel McCaden frowned thoughtfully. "Riley McCaden ya' say. Well, the names the same, no doubt. But I don't think we're related. Unless ya' just arrived from my beloved Ireland?"

Riley shook his head. "No sir."

Daniel shook his head. "Well then lad, ya' can't be family, for it is only me and my wife who's here. Other Irish folks yes, but I can assure ya', there have been no other McCadens." Daniel sighed, making a face. "If this be a prank you're pullin' I haven't the time, there are far too many things to be gettin' done. Now if it's a handout you 're needin', I'll be glad to give ya' a bite to eat, then you'll have to be gettin' on your way."

Riley hesitated, thinking. The pause made his great, great grandfather sigh again. Shaking his head, he began to close the door, but Riley yelled out in desperation.

"No! Please. This is no joke. I, we, need your help."

Daniel's green eyes widened, sweeping over them both. "All right lads," he said, "I'll give ya' time to explain what's goin' on, but ya' best be makin' it good." Daniel opened the door wide and let them in. They followed him to a heavy wooden table with benches and sat.

Riley glanced around. The room was both a storage and work area. Shelves covered every wall, all of them stacked with glass bottles, various sized wooden boxes, and a few large crates not yet opened. On a long bench lay a collection of glass tubing and beakers, obviously used for mixing and calculating medicines. Riley brought his wandering eyes back to his great, great grandfather.

Daniel McCaden was taller than Riley expected, about the same age as his Dad, around forty or so, and was wide across the shoulders. His fists were big and his arms powerful. But his green eyes showed kindness. There was caution in them, but they sparkled with a willingness to listen.

In the middle of the table a lantern burned with a low flame. Daniel turned up the wick and the area brightened. "Now," he said soberly, "tell me of this help ya' need."

Riley glanced at Bowdie and got a shrug. So he moved his eyes back to his great, great grandfather. Slowly, step by step, Riley started at the beginning. He explained about Bowdie and Michaela, the old mansion and his search there. He told of the trunk and of Casey and Frog and Harvey and Mr. Climers. He described the TT-V and their horrible ride back to 1888. He told of the map and about Professor Hale holding the key to its whereabouts, how different this period in history was and how scary it seemed to them. And he told of his Dad tracing the family history and of the old photos in his collection.

Quietly Daniel McCaden took it all in with a face that gave no indication of what he was thinking. Bowdie, like Riley, sat silent watching him, praying he'd believe. Bowdie also thought one other thing; how cool it was that Riley had traveled back in time and was actually talking face to face with own great, great grandfather; a man who had already been dead well over a hundred years.

CHAPTER THIRTY-TWO

Considering the extraordinary story he had just been told, Daniel McCaden said nothing and stared into the lamp's yellow flame. The room was quiet and they heard the muffled click of horse hoofs clopping down the brick street out front.

Somewhere in the city a church bell rang. The moment was tense. A fly buzzed passed Bowdie's ear and landed on the table near the base of the lamp. Bowdie watched it walk a short distance than fly away.

Daniel McCaden turned to face them. The red headed Irishman cleared his throat and folded his hands, laying them to rest on the table top. He spoke slowly, choosing his words carefully. "I don't know, lads" he said shaking his head, "tis like a fairy-tale you're tellin'. Do ya' have any proof?"

Something had to be thought of quick, before his own great, great grandfather threw them out into the streets. Swiftly Riley climbed to his feet. "Look!" he said excitedly, "look at my clothes, at my shoes, they're Nike's. You don't have these yet, they're not invented."

Daniel glanced at the sneakers but still shook his head. "I'll admit lad, tis' a shoe I've never seen, but this world is filled with things my Irish eyes have never looked upon." Riley grew sick to his stomach. Daniel looked into each of their faces, "Lads," he said, "I'm sorry, but ya' failed to convince me. I believe ya' come only to make a fool of me."

Bowdie suddenly clapped his hands and jumped up from the table dancing like a pro football Player who'd just made a touchdown. Parading around in circles he yelled, "I got it, I got it, I got it." Digging into his pocket he pulled out the quarter he had once offered Casey for a candy bar. He handed it to Riley's great, great grandfather. "Here, Mr. McCaden" he said, voice on fire with confidence, "look at it, check out the date, read the year and you'll believe."

Daniel McCaden held the coin flat in the palm of his hand staring at Bowdie, then lowered his eyes to the quarter. He moved in toward the light of the lamp. Across the top of the coin he read the word LIBERTY and below it recognized the impression of George Washington. Then he read the words IN GOD WE TRUST.

Seconds passed and to Riley and Bowdie they were agonizing. The room remained still and quiet. Daniel's words were little more than a mumble when he finally spoke. Slowly he stood to his feet, "Blessed Mary Mother of God, 2021."

"Yeah," Bowdie burst with excitement, "it's two years before, but it's from our time."

Slowly Daniel lowered his hand and with a nod gave Bowdie a warm smile. Then, holding his smile turned his green eyes to Riley. Riley grinned back; noticing his great, great grandfather was chewing on his bottom lip. *Just like me!* Riley thought.

Daniel McCaden' s smile widened. It was a big smile and with it came the words Riley and Bowdie both wanted to hear. "Well you've done it lads," he said, "ya' made me a believer."

They rose from the table and the boys shouted out loud. Daniel McCaden pulled his great, great grandson into his arms, then grabbed Bowdie and pulled him in too, squeezing them both tight. Neither of the boys saw it, but the smile on Daniel McCaden' s face grew even bigger.

CHAPTER THIRTY-THREE

The three sat around the table trying to come up with a plan. The lantern light was soft and comfortable, but reminded Riley of just how far away from home they were.

With even Daniel in the mix, many of the same doubts arose: would they even be allowed to visit Professor Hale? And if so, could they convince him to tell where the map was hidden? If close, and thy recovered it immediately, then they could catch the TT-V upon its return twenty-four hours from now; Riley looked at his watch, actually twenty-one hours and sixteen minutes from now. But if the map was far away - then what, travel in1888 took a long time. Could they get to it, take possession and return before July 22?

Daniel had brewed a pot of tea and served it with freshly baked bread. Riley and Bowdie smothered the slices with homemade blackberry jelly and ate heartily. By the time they were finished a plan had been decided.

They would wait for the sun to go down and the judge to return home. At that time they would carry tea and bread to the jail and present it to Professor Hale as a last meal offering. Surely, even the hardest of jail guards would not deny a condemned man his last meal, or his last late-night snack.

At 6:30 p.m. they put together a basket, locked the store and walked to the courthouse. The jail cells would be in the basement.

Long dark clouds lined with fading sunlight painted the western sky. The streets were nearly deserted, and the city lay quiet. A soft breeze ruffled their hair. Climbing the courthouse steps they entered the building. Its emptiness magnified the echoing of their every footstep. At the north stairway leading to the basement they started down. All were nervous; everything depended upon Professor Hale's cooperation.

At the bottom they found a guard sitting behind a well-worn desk. As they approached he stood and smiled briefly. He was an older man like Casey, but this fellow sported a gray bushy mustache and was nearly bald. He was dressed in a red shirt with black suspenders holding up a pair of faded jeans.

"What might your business be" he asked.

Daniel held up the basket, "Food for Professor Hale, tis Christian charity."

The old guard nodded. "That' right nice of you, Irishman. But you won't mind if I have a look-see will you?"

Daniel smiled. "Not a bit. In fact, while you're at it, why don't ya' be havin' yourself a piece of bread and jelly too."

The guard checked it thoroughly, helped himself to the offering then handed the basket back. "You say it's Hale you're wanting?"

Daniel nodded. "I."

Behind the guard was a wooden door with a small, barred window. Pulling a ring of keys from the desk drawer the old guard unlocked it. Then moving aside said, "Last cell on the left. Have your selves a nice visit. When you want out just give me a yell. I'll be locking the door behind you."

Daniel nodded again and they walked through. The door closed and the keys jingled as he locked them in. It was a feeling the boys did not like. They stood in a long corridor with cells on both sides. Hurrying to Hale's location they stopped and stared; surprised at what they saw.

CHAPTER THRITY-FOUR

Professor Hale was a frail old man. Sitting on the edge of a wooden cot he looked up. His eyes were sunken and his face thin. Slumped over, he sat with a blanket wrapped tightly around him. After coughing several times he spoke with a weak voice. "Yes, what is it you want?"

Daniel spoke first. "We're sorry to be botherin' ya' Professor, but these young lads are in great need of your help." Daniel raised the basket of bread and jelly, "and we've brought ya' a snack."

Professor Hale looked at the basket and shook his head no. Then asked, "How is it you need my help, I'm being hung tomorrow? I couldn't be of help to anyone."

Riley gripped the bars with his hands. "That's not true sir, we do need your help very much."

Hale's brow wrinkled with curiosity. "And how might that be?" He asked.

"It's a long story."

"Then you best hurry," Hale replied, "I've but a short time left."

Riley blurted it out. "We need to know where the other half of the map is."

Professor Hale's eyes narrowed, he stared at Riley for several seconds then rose to his feet. Anger brought life back into his voice. "Did that poor excuse of a judge send you?"

"Judge Murda, you mean?" Riley asked.

"Of course I mean Murda." Hale snapped.

"No sir." Riley explained. "We don't like him anymore than you do. It's just that without the other half of the map, Bowdie and I have no chance at all of ever getting back home."

Hale glanced at Bowdie, than Daniel and back to Riley. "And where's home?"

Riley stared at the Professor, wondering if he should tell the whole story.

But Daniel cut in. "I'll not be lyin' to ya' Professor, the boys live a good ways from here. Without that map, they'll never be seein' their parents or home again."

"So you're telling me the truth, then?" Hale asked looking at Riley and Bowdie.

Both boys nodded. After several long seconds, Hale turned away and walked to the far side of the cell where he stood with his back to them. Riley started to say something, but Daniel put a finger to his lips.

Impatiently they waited, wanting to hurry the Professor along. This was so important! He just had to help. If he didn't, all would be over.

Despite it being evening with the sun going down, the cell block was still hot. Riley felt himself sweating. Closing his eyes he prayed in silence for God's help, asking He touch the Professor' heart and help him to understand.

Finally after several long minutes of silence, Hale walked to where they stood. Still holding the blanket about his shoulders he spoke calmly. "I am going to tell you for two reasons. First: in my heart I feel you're telling me the truth. And second, I have nothing to lose, I'm dying anyway. The secret would only go the grave with me."

Bowdie had a sudden thought and blurted it out, "Professor Hale, I've got the coolest John Wayne idea." Everyone looked at him, waiting. "We'll break you out. Than you can take us right to the map yourself. You won't have to hang tomorrow. You can disappear across the border into Mexico or Canada!"

Riley agreed quietly to himself but remembered what Mr. Climers had told Frog about not changing history. If Professor Hale did not hang it could alter the future somehow. So as much as he wanted to help the Professor, he knew it would be both wrong and dangerous.

Professor Hale gave Bowdie a warm smile. "Thank you for the kind offer young man, but it's not logical. Such a move would only make criminals out of the lot of you. Besides, I'm old and dying of Tuberculosis. I won't even see another month anyway." He paused to get his breath, "the hanging will only end my agony a little sooner."

The Professor began coughing, this time violently. He spit up a large amount of blood, wiping his mouth with a handkerchief. When under control he adjusted the blanket and spoke in a watchful whisper. "It will require travel. The map is at my sister's house in Tucson."

"Arizona?" Riley asked.

Hale nodded. "Yes. 648 Forest Street. You'll find it hidden in the north wall of her bedroom behind a painting of four running horses. Her home is adobe, and you must pull a brick away and reach in, it will be there. Tell her Bob sent you." He paused, looked down at his feet than back to Riley. "And son, when you see her, tell her I love her."

Riley smiled for the old Professor. "I'll tell her, I promise. We will never forget you. I wish there was something we could do."

"Yeah," Bowdie said, "Just name it."

Hale coughed then replied, "Just get your selves home safely."

Daniel gave the Professor an appreciative nod and they turned to leave.

Hale called after them. "A word of warning," stopping they turned to face him. "If you use the map and go into the cities," he said, "enter with caution. There is a legend of four Angels: the Angels of Death. It's said they roam the streets in search of anyone who would enter to steal and plunder. It's told they breathe death from their mouths." He coughed again, "I urge you not to go in, but if you must, take a red cloth and tie it over your nose and mouth when the Angels come; it is said their breath cannot penetrate a cloth of red."

The old Professor fell silent than ending their conversation with a nod. Daniel thanked him and the three walked away.

They left the courthouse and stepped outside into the now dark night. Stars hung in the sky and a full moon shimmered across the surface of the Wabash River. Around them, the city of Lafayette 1888 stood quiet and only a few of the buildings showed signs of light. Although dim, the glow of gas lamps lined the city streets. It was decided they would spend the night at Daniel's house and rethink their plan in the morning.

The wooden sidewalks clicked beneath Riley's great, great grandfather's boot heals, and the noise made him realize yet once again, they were far from home and not in their own time.

It was obvious they would not be returning within the twenty-four-hour period. Now they would have to wait for the July 22 trip. Riley also knew that sometime during the night Frog would visit Professor Hale and probably gain the same information they did. That would mean a race getting to Tucson, acquiring the map and rushing back to catch the TT-V before he did. If they missed the 22nd trip, they would be stuck here forever.

Could they do it? Riley wondered. Could he and Bowdie who knew nothing about surviving in 1888, travel thousands of miles to Arizona, take possession of a map worth tillions of dollars, than get back to hurdle themselves through time and negotiate for their lives? And could it be done without running into Frog?

Riley gazed up into the stars. They were bright and twinkled like a million glowing candles. It all looked so peaceful he thought, but like the year of 2023, those stars were so very far away.

CHAPTER THIRTY-FIVE

Even in the moonlight his grandmother's house looked very much the same. Riley felt excitement as they climbed the steps to the front-door; the very steps he had climbed hundreds of times. At least the house, he thought, was something familiar in the way things used to be; although in 2023 the place was just one of many in a long line of others. Here in 1888 it sat by itself.

Riley's great, great grandmother Marie met them at the door when they walked in. She was young and pretty, with red hair falling to below her shoulders. Her eyes were bright blue, and she reminded Riley of his Mom. He liked her immediately. After giving Daniel a kiss on the cheek Marie McCaden smiled, redirecting her attention to Riley and Bowdie. "And who might it be you've brought home this time, Daniel McCaden?" She asked.

Daniel slipped an arm around his wife' and looked at the boys. "That one," he said pointing at Bowdie, "Is young Bowdie Pager." Bowdie waved a hand shyly. "And the other lad my love, is Riley McCaden." Marie gave her husband a quick glance then looked back at Riley. "Really," She said cheerfully, "Is he a relative, then?"

Daniel nodded. "I. The lad is your great, great grandson." Marie turned and teasingly slapped Daniel's shoulder. "Ah, don't be makin' such jokes now husband. Honestly, who might the handsome lad be?"

"No. I swear it to be true, Marie. As difficult as it is to be believin' he comes to us from the future, the year 2023 to be exact." Marie's mouth opened with surprise and her forehead wrinkled with confusion. Daniel smiled at her. "Ya' best believe me woman. And ya' might want to be closen' your mouth or you'll be swallowin' a fly." Daniel winked at Bowdie, "put the coin in her hand, lad."

Bowdie pulled the quarter from his pocket and handed it to Marie. As she examined it everyone waited anxiously for her reaction. When her eyes lifted she looked at Bowdie first, than Riley, "Sure as the good Lord lives in Heaven," she said feeling the shock of it, "you're not pullin' my leg, are ya' Daniel?" He really is who ya' say."

"I, wife, he really is." Daniel kissed her on the cheek, "Now, my love," he added rubbing his hands together as if they were cold, "if you'll be fixin' us some tea and a bite to eat, we'll be sittin' down and fillin' ya' in as to what's goin' on."

Daniel and the boys headed for the living room while Marie hurried off to the kitchen talking out-loud to herself "my great, great grandson, here from the future." Her face brightened with a smile as she added, "and Riley McCaden. Tis' a name I like."

Marie retuned with a tray of four cups, silverware, pot of tea and a big chocolate cake. Riley and Bowdie could hardly wait. As soon as everyone was served they explained everything, each sharing their part of the story. Marie listened with excitement sitting on the edge of her chair. It was as if she were listening to a wondrous fairy-tale.

They talked a long while. Hours passed as they told of life in their-own period of history. Daniel and Marie smiled at the boy's reaction when they told of priming and working the hand-pump in the kitchen each time they needed water. And when they explained there was no indoor plumbing that they used an outhouse during the day and chamber pots at night, Bowdie wrinkled his nose. Hesitantly he asked, "I know what an outhouse is," he said, "but what's a chamber pot?"

Hiding his smile, Daniel explained. "They are pots ya' go to the bathroom in at night, then empty and washout the next day."

Bowdie's wrinkled nose tuned into a shocked face. "You use them for both number one and number two?"

Daniel gave a nod. "I, which ever one ya' have need of doin'."

Looking nervous, Bowdie glanced at Riley and back to Daniel, "Um, just out of curiosity, who's responsible for emptying them?"

Daniel looked at Marie pretending to be surprised, then glanced soberly back at Bowdie. "Tis a courtesy lad, always they are emptied by your house guests." Bowdie's eyes grew big, and Daniel burst into laughter. He looked at Marie again, than brought his self under control. "No, Bowdie," he said smiling, "Tis' only kidding I do. I am the one who empties the pots."

Flushing with embarrassment Bowdie told him. "Oh. Well I was just wondering, Mr. McCaden, that's all."

CHAPTER THIRTY-SIX

The chatting and sharing continued. Marie and Daniel talked about their smokehouse; explaining that was how they preserved meat. They explained the importance of ice and how they frequently purchased huge blocks of it to keep things cold and food from spoiling. Faces warm with memories; they spoke of Ireland, its beauty, its people, and the family still there; of their four children waiting to come over, staying with Marie's parents until arrangements could be made.

They told of their dangerous and crowded voyage to America by ship; of the rough seas and terrible storms encountered. They explained the lack of food and water to drink and about the great need of medicine; of the abundant sickness and death among passengers and crew. And when they explained the trip took weeks to cross the sea, the boys imagined how terrible it really must have been.

Then realizing they were doing all the talking, Daniel and Marie apologized and asked the boys to tell of life and the wonders of the future. Marie refilled their tea cups and she and Daniel listened with astonishment.

Riley and Bowdie told them of speeding automobiles, Greyhound buses, and Amtrak Trains. They explained what an airplane was and how it could easily fly them all to Ireland in only a few hours. Daniel and Marie shook their heads, finding it almost impossible to imagine such things.

Taking turns the boys told them about movies, television and radio, gas and electric stoves, and microwaves. They spoke of giant shopping malls, huge stores such as Wall-mart, Marsh and Meijer's, of computers and fast-food restaurants. Riley told his great, great grandfather about modern day Drugstores, called Pharmacies, and about industrial automation; how giant machines operated by a single person could mass produce thousands of products a day. Daniel McCaden sat in awe.

And so the talk went, running on for hours. It was Marie who realized the time and put an end to it. "We've done enough talkin' for one night," she told everyone, "tis time for bed."

Lighting a lamp she led the boys to a bedroom upstairs. There were different furnishings now, but it was the very room Riley slept in when staying over with his grandmother growing up. The room possessed a happy feeling of familiarity, yet it also reinforced their dreadful situation.

After placing the lamp on a dresser Marie pulled down the covers of a big bed near the window. "There," she said facing the boys with a smile, "you'll sleep well tonight, and in the mornin' I'll be cookin' a breakfast fit for an Irish King."

Daniel was standing at the door leaned against the frame. Agreeing, he spoke up with a reassuring smile. "I. And tomorrow while we eat, we'll be plannin' a trip to Arizona." Riley and Bowdie looked at one another smiling.

Marie gave them a hug and kissed the tops of their head. "Now sleep tight," she said, "and don't be lettin' the bedbugs bite."

Bowdie looked worriedly at Riley. Marie saw it and grinned. "No Bowdie, you need not be worryin', we got no bedbugs, tis just an old sayin', a rhyme. Now get yourselves into bed and sleep well." She and Daniel left, closing the door quietly behind them.

The lamp was still on the dresser, so Riley turned it low, then they undressed and climbed into bed. The lamp's soft glow covered the room with shadows. Bowdie rolled onto his side and yawned. When finished he asked, Riley "you don't really think there are bedbugs in here with us, do you?"

Riley laughed, "No, you worrywart. My dad use to say the same thing to me all the time. Now go to sleep."

Bowdie yawned again, rolling again onto his back. "You're sure about the Bed Bug thing?"

"Yes I'm sure, you Caveman Dingle Berry."

Bowdie frowned, "Okay, What's a Dingle Berry?"

"Riley laughed, "it's those tiny little smelly things that hang off the hair on your butt when you don't have any toilet paper.

Bowdie made a face, "Riley McCaden that's sick. Your such a dork!

Riley laughed again, "Yep, now go to sleep. I assure you there are no Bed Bugs!"

"And you are absolutely sure?"

"Yes Bowdie Pager, absolutely sure."

Bowdie snickered, "As sure as you are at checking a pulse and pronouncing the person is dead?"

Riley kicked Bowdie beneath the covers. "Shut up and go to sleep you poop face!"

"Oh", Bowdie said, "so now I have Dingle Berries on my face!"

Riley sighed out loud, "Just shut up and go to sleep".

Smiling into the soft shadows of the oil lamp, Bowdie rolled over, nestled his head into his pillow and closed his eyes. He loved his best friend. A peaceful slumber came quickly.

But Riley couldn't sleep. Lying on his back he laced his fingers behind his head and stared into the dark ceiling. So much had happened in such a short time. Only hours ago he had left the tent in his backyard to search for Bowdie. Now, here they were a hundred and forty years into the past, sleeping in a strange bed at the home of his great, great grandfather; a man who should be long dead, and the TT-V…a Time Machine; such things only existed in the movies and in books written by creative writers like King, Koontz and Rice.

Riley chewed on his lip as he sighed, wondering if he and Bowdie would ever see home again? They were fortunate to be here with family and that was certainly a blessing. But as thankful as he was, his great, great grandparents were not his mom and dad, and this was not 2023.

Tomorrow they would be leaving for Arizona to get the map; that was a great relief. But even that had a dark side; Frog might already be on his way there. And if he got to it first, they were doomed.

Outside the window crickets chirped loud and a full moon covered the earth in silver light. The stars continued to brighten the heavens, but Riley made a face; they were the same stars shining over his mom and dad.

Yawning, he turned onto his side too. The night was growing chilly and the blankets that covered them felt warm. Without realizing, sleep crept in and Riley began to dream; he was home and at a wedding; the wedding of Bowdie and Michaela. And to his shock, Bowdie's best man, of all people, was Mr. Climers.

The Rock was the Pastor and Bowdie was residing his vows to Michaela…*and I promise forever to bow before you, to do all the housework, change all the baby's diapers. And come rain, hail, snow, or deadly streaks of lightening, I will paint your name on a different wall at Murda Mansion every day of my life. And I solemnly swear you are now my best friend.*

The dream didn't end; then suddenly bells were ringing, and the happy couple were charging down the church steps smiling and laughing, running to a horse-drawn carriage waiting at the curve.

The driver was Judge Murda dressed in his black robe. After assisting the bride and groom into the carriage he turned to Riley and pointed to a tree from which hung two hangman's nooses. Riley yelled "NO" and it woke him up.

Sitting straight up he panicked at first, but quickly realized where he was and that he had been dreaming. Twisting to look at Bowdie he caught his breath, Bowdie was gone!

The voice came from near the door, "Looking for your girlfriend you little sissy? Steeped in shadows the face of the speaker was impossible to distinguish. But there was no mistaking the voice. It was Frog.

CHAPTER THIRTY-SEVEN

Frog was holding Bowdie by the hair with one hand and holding a knife to his throat with the other. Although he couldn't see the fat man's face, Riley could imagine its evil expression of pleasure.

Frog spoke again, making a game of it, "Just think you little twerp, one slip and it's all over for the chocolate kid, here. You yell one time and I'll cut out his Adam's apple then make you eat it. You're taking me to the map. And I promise, if even one time you make a run for it, or lie to me, we'll flip a coin and the looser will be sliced, diced and left for the buzzards. Now get out of that bed and dress."

Riley slipped into his clothes wondering what he should do. He wanted to yell out for great, great grandfather Daniel; he could take Frog. But long before he reached them Bowdie would lie dead. So like it or not, he had no choice…at least for now.

Frog spoke again always making sure he kept his voice low. Riley tied his Nike's as Frog talked. "I know you two met with the Professor. And I know he told you the map was hidden in Arizona. The old geezer wouldn't tell me where," Frog shrugged, "but I got to give him credit though; he was a tough old bird, never screamed once."

Riley stopped tying his Nikes and looked at Frog. "You better not have hurt him."

Frog smirked. "Stop, you're scaring me you little flea. So what if I did. What are you going to do about it?" Riley didn't answer. Really, what could he do about it? He wasn't big enough to fight Frog. He finished tying his sneakers and stood.

Frog turned Bowdie loose and ordered him to get dressed too, then walked to the bed grabbing a corner of the sheet. He cut a long, narrow strip and when Bowdie was dressed, he bound their wrists together, "There," he said in his deep, disgusting voice, "now if one runs the other will have to run with him, slowing you down and making you an easy catch."

Moving to the door he opened it slightly and peered out into the hall. The house was quiet and dark. Glancing over his shoulder he whispered to Riley, "Your great, great gramps is certainly a trusting soul. He left the front door unlocked for me. I walked right in. Now remember, if either of you make so much as a peep, it's over for everybody. Frog put away his knife and pulled his revolver. "I mean over EVERYBODY! Understand?"

The boys nodded. With Frog right behind, they made their way down the stairs and out into the night. The early morning air was cold. There was no need to ask where they were going.

CHAPTER THIRTY-EIGHT

With sadness Riley glanced back at the house. It was draped in moonlight and inside its familiar shadows, asleep, laid their only hope. Now because of this fat, greedy evil man, there was none. Daniel and Marie McCaden were his great, great grandparents and he wished he could have told them goodbye.

Frog kicked Riley in the rear. "Turn around you turd-maggot before I rip out one of your eyes. You won't ever see them again, anyway, so quite acting like a home sick little school girl. I suppose next you'll start crying and begging; 'oh please Mr. Frog, let me go give granny and grampy a kissie, kissie goodbye'."

Riley bit at his lip to keep from telling Frog what he thought. But expressing his anger just didn't seem the right thing to do; not now, not to a Frog Crooking Creep maniac carrying a knife and a gun.

They marched downtown to the train depot where they waited inside sitting on hard wood benches. The fat man purchased three tickets to Chicago and one newspaper. As he read, the boys sat quiet, wondering if a run for it was worth the risk. It felt like the right thing to do, but if Frog caught them it would mean a guaranteed death sentence for at least one of them. Besides, neither could outrun a bullet.

Time passed slowly and occasionally when Frog turned a page, his coat moved just enough to expose his shoulder holster. They knew he would not hesitate to shoot anyone who got in the way of getting the map.

At 5:00am they heard the train whistle blow. Frog folded his paper and stuck it under his arm. He then hurried the boys outside to the loading dock. The sky was beginning to lighten. There were three others waiting for the train: an old lady in a black dress and hat holding a large handbag, a Priest in robes and a young man in a dark sweater with a giant white "P" across the back.

The group watched the train approached. The engine was loud and the noise irritating to the ears. A huge smokestack belched white clouds and the whistle sounded until the train lurched to a stop.

The two passenger cars pulled behind the engine looked like rectangular boxes sitting on large iron wheels. Through their long line of windows Riley and Bowdie watched as hanging lanterns swayed to a standstill, causing shadows to swish over the hard, non-padded bench seats. Bowdie looked at Riley, "lucky us, Amtrak 1888."

Frog slapped Bowdie in the back of the head, "shut your pie hole."

A conductor dressed in black stepped out from the front coach waving a lantern, "All aboard for Chicago." He held the lamp for light as everyone boarded.

Directing the boys to the back of the coach Frog sat them together in the seat in front of him.

The whistle blew again, and the train jerked forward. This was it Riley thought; his great, great grandfather was not coming to the rescue; now he and Bowdie were for sure on their own. Tiredly, he laid his head against the back of the seat. There was no question, they had to get away somehow; get away without getting caught.

The train steamed its way to Chicago. It was a noisy ride made worse by the endless rocking. The seats were hard and the tiny bathroom smelled as if Frog had pushed their head down through the round wooden hole where everyone relieved themselves. The horrible, smelly collection of poop and pee splashed and swashed with each rock of the coach. There was no air-conditioning, and the open widows were the only cool air available. There was one good thing however: the countryside looked much the way it did in 2008, with scattered farms, planted fields and grazing animals.

At Chicago they caught another train that took them to St. Louis, from there to Denver, down to Albuquerque, over the Arizona line and across the Mohave Desert. Five days after leaving Lafayette, the train's whistle announced their arrival at the city of Tucson.

It had been five days of sleeping on hardwood seats, eating once a day, and going without a bath. They smelled worse than road-killed Skunks, and Frog was in great need of a shave; but worse of all, he Frog could have used a good half-hour worth of time brushing his teeth and gargling with a full bottle of mouthwash. The two couldn't decide which would have been worse...skinned-alive by his knife, shot in the gut by his gun, or him throwing them to the floor, sitting on them and repeatedly breathing in their face. Bowdie had wrenched at the thought. He even confessed the unbelievable, admitting he'd have traded Michaela for a shower and a good meal.

When they stepped off the train and onto the platform, Riley and Bowdie stared in awe. It was like a scene right out of an HBO Western Movie in high definition.

Cowboys on horseback strolled leisurely down main street, buckboards ambled by, and two huge, covered wagons sat unhitched near a big barn with a sign that read, MULEY'S BLACKSMITH & LIVERY.

Not every man wore a gun on his hip, but most were dressed in Blue Jeans, Shirt, Boots and wearing Cowboy Hats. Horses were tied to hitching posts everywhere, and the city had every kind of business imaginable. There was a store called The Tucson Mercantile, a huge Hotel, a Law Office, a two-story Newspaper Building, four Saloons, two Restaurants, a Dress Maker, and a Doctor's Office: all within sight of the train depot. Streets stretched off in all directions.

Caught up in the idea of being in a real-live western town here in the 1800's, Riley and Bowdie felt a twinge of excitement. But Frog put an end to it, "Quite you're gawking girls," he said, chewing on a cigar, "we're here on business."v

CHAPTER THIRTY-NINE

During the trip Riley had told Frog the address of Professor Hale's sister and about the picture in her bedroom. He had done so reluctantly. But Frog was intent on getting the map and to refuse would have meant his hurting Bowdie.

The house was located in the south part of town. And just as Professor Hale had said, it was made of adobe. It sat at the end of the street beneath the shade of a tall bushy Oak tree. There was a blue picket fence around the yard and a little white puppy on the other side. Wagging its tail it watched them approach.

When they walked through the gate it waddled up to greet them. But mumbling his dislike for animals Frog used his foot to kick it away. Yelping, it scurried away beneath the house. Bowdie looked angrily at Frog, "Man, you're a horse's…" Bowdie didn't finish the word; Frog slapped the side of his head. "Shut up."

At the porch Frog pounded on the door then looked down at the boys. "I'll do the talking. Open your traps without me saying it's okay, and it'll be over for the both of you, and her too. Got it?" The boys nodded and the door opened.

Professor Hale's sister was elderly. Her hair was gray and lay tied in a bun on top of her head. She wore round glasses and a black cooking apron spotted with flour wrapped around her brown dress. Her voice was soft and kind.

"Yes. May I help you?" She looked at Frog first then at Bowdie and Riley with a smile. Frog pulled his hat from his head like a gentleman. Riley and Bowdie rolled their eyes.

"Yes mam'," he said, "you can in deed help me. My name is William F. Norris. I'm a Private Investigator with the Pinkerton Agency in Chicago." She gave a nod with an expression that said go on. "Your brother, Robert, in Lafayette, Indiana, sent me."

"Oh," She said with surprise.

"Yes" Frog lied. "It's a delicate matter, may we come in?"

"Certainly" She opened the door and led them to the living room. Frog and the boys sat on a sofa and she in a rocker. "Please excuse the way I look," she apologized, "but I've been baking. Now please, tell me about Bob. Is he in some sort of trouble?"

Frog replied immediately. "No not at all. He's fine, enjoying his job at the College."

"Then why are you here?"

"To be frank, he has sent me after the map."

She stared at Frog, surprised at what he had just said. Then she moved her eyes to the boys. "What's the story with these two?" She asked.

Frog faked a grin. "Them. Oh, they're just a couple of runaways I'm returning to Chicago. Double duty if you know what I mean."

Professor Hale's sister laced her fingers and laid her hands in her lap. "Why does Robert want the map, Mr. Norris?"

"He has promised it to a museum in Indianapolis. I'm to ensure it gets there safely."

"I see," she said thoughtfully, "well quite frankly, I'm afraid I don't have it."

Frog's face flushed and he snapped. "That's crap you wrinkled prune. You're lying right through those old-bitty teeth. It's in your bedroom behind the painting."

The woman's expression showed her surprise. Frog laughed at her while climbing to his feet. He grabbed the boys by the collar, "Come on you horse-turds. Let's go have a look see."

CHAPTER FORTY

With a powerful grip on the boys, Frog stormed the house until he found the bedroom with the picture of the four horses. Forcing Riley and Bowdie down on the edge of the bed he grinned excitedly.

Professor Hale's sister had followed them in and sat beside the boys. Frog jerked the painting off the wall tossing it to the floor. A loose brick lay right behind, just as the Professor had said. Working it free he threw it down on top of the painting, than crammed his fat hand into the hole. When he pulled it out, it was empty…no map!

Spinning around he pulled his gun from its holster and grabbed the old lady by the arm, pulling her up from the bed. Teeth gritted; he waved the gun in her face. "Old bag, I didn't come here to play. I want that map, and I want it now."

She was a brave woman. "I'll make you a deal, Mr. Norris, or whatever your real name is."

Frog tightened his grip and she gasped. "I don't make deals." He said. "Where's the map?"

"I'm afraid you have no choice, Mr. Norris," she told him trying to ignore the pain he was causing, "it's a deal or just kill me now and never know. At my age, dying doesn't frighten me."

Frog cursed and released her. "Alright, what's the deal?"

Rubbing her arm she spoke calmly. "I tell you where the map is in exchange for the boys."

For several seconds Frog gave it consideration, "We'll compromise," he said, "and you'll accept it, or I swear; I'll be the only one leaving this house alive." Seeing the evil in his eyes she agreed to listen. "You tell me where the map is hidden, and I'll leave one of the boys with you, and take one with me, that's it."

Riley and Bowdie remained silent. Professor Hale's sister stared at Frog a long while. She knew the outlook for the boy he took would not be good, but there was simply no other way. "Okay," she said, "you take one of them with you, but he's to be set free as soon as you have the map in your possession."

Frog laughed. "Sure. Now where is it?"

She took a deep breath. "It's in Tombstone, hidden in a room above the Crystal Palace Saloon. I'll not tell you the room number now. Go there and ask for the barkeep they call, Piller. Tell him to send a telegram to me stating that the boy is safe. I in return will send a gram back giving you the exact location." She fell silent then, waiting for his reaction.

Frog stared hard at her. "Okay," he said finally. "But heed my warning. You cross me and it's over for the kid. Then I come back here for you and the other one, understand?"

She nodded and Frog turned to the boys still sitting on the bed. "Now," he said with a twisted grin, "which one of you would like to take a fun trip to Tombstone with friendly Mr. Frog?"

Riley and Bowdie spoke at the same time… "I'll go." They looked at one another. Inside neither wanted to go. They were both equally frightened. But Riley knew how much Frog hated Bowdie, and he feared the fat man would kill him no matter what. Bowdie on the other hand was thinking Riley was in this mess in the first place because of him. Going with Frog was a way of making it up to him.

Placing his gun back into the holster Frog pulled his knife and cut the bond holding the boys together. He then glared at the old lady. "One more thing, don't you even think about calling the law. If I even see the shadow of a lawman, the boy dies." He then grabbed Bowdie by the collar and pulled him roughly through the house and out the front door. The old lady and Riley followed quickly behind, stopping on the porch.

At the gate Frog paused and looked at Riley. "If you know what's good for your friend, don't even consider following. Your usefulness has just run out." He pulled Bowdie along and they disappeared down the street.

Riley's lower lip began to quiver, and he held it between his teeth. That fat heartless killer had Bowdie, with no one to stop him from doing whatever he wanted. Something had to be done.

Riley started off the porch but Professor Hale's sister grabbed his arm. "No," she said, "he's not bluffing. You go after them and he'll kill your friend for sure, than take you in his place."

Riley knew she was right. He stared across the empty yard fearing he would never see his best friend again. Helplessness washed over him, and wetness filled his eyes. Professor Hale's sister slipped an arm around him. "You've got to be strong" she told him, "this is one of those times we've just got to thrust in the Lord."

Down the street from the Blacksmith's shop the ring of a hammer pounding medal on an iron anvil filled the air. Then Riley realized the little puppy was barking. Glancing down he realized it was standing at his feet with tail wagging. Picking him up, he kissed it on the top of the head. *At least there was somebody, he thought, happy in this world.*

CHAPTER FORTY-ONE

Professor Hale's sister, who asked to be called Margaret, had Riley carry the puppy into the house. She heated water and used most of it to fill an old brass tub, then gave Riley a bar of soap and a wink.

While he bathed she washed his clothes and hung them to dry. The old tub wasn't a shower, but Riley savored the feel of being clean again. When finished, he wrapped himself in the heavy wool blanket Margaret had set out.

For supper she warmed up stew and biscuits; the best he ever tasted. While eating, he filled her in on all that was happening. She understood his worry over Bowdie and assured him her friend Pillar was a tough character. He would do everything in his power to keep Bowdie safe.

With difficulty, Riley changed the subject explaining Professor Hale's situation in Indiana. Margaret accepted it nobly while hiding the pain it caused. But when he told her his last words were that he loved her: tears filled her eyes and she wept.

Feeling uneasy; worried he may have done the wrong thing by telling her, Riley reached across the table and held her hand, "Remember what you told me" he said "you have to be strong."

Sniffling, Margaret gave his hand a squeeze and wiped at her eyes. She smiled, "Yes Riley, you're right. I should practice what I preach. And thank you for telling me, it meant a great deal."

Night came quickly and brought with it a chill. Margaret built a fire and Riley welcomed the warmth. He lay on the sofa staring into the flames with the puppy curled beside him.

Little by little his troubled mind eased as sleep slowly swept over him. Margaret covered him with another blanket and kissed his forehead. She then sat quietly in her rocker and read by the firelight.

Outside, the town of Tucson Arizona 1888 began calling it a night. Houses went dark, the streets thinned with people and businesses stood dark and locked. Except for the noisy saloons, Tucson lay lost to the desert's vastness.

It was nearly midnight when the knock on the door startled Margaret awake. She too had drifted off. Glancing at Riley still asleep, she rose, grabbed a pistol and made her way to the door.

Upon returning, she knelled beside Riley's sleeping form and shook him gently. Opening his eyes he looked at her, than up at the man standing behind her. It was Daniel McCaden. Riley scrambled from the couch and the two embraced; a new hope rising in Riley's heart.

After warming a bowl of the stew for Daniel, Margaret explained about Bowdie being with Frog and about her friend Piller in Tombstone. Daniel understood Frog was crazy and would not hesitate to harm Bowdie. They had to move fast. Daniel looked at Riley, "are ya' up to a hard ride through the desert, lad?"

"Will it mean getting Bowdie back?" Riley asked waiting for the answer he so needed to hear.

Daniel winked. "I. We'll be gettin' him back. The lad has a way of growin' on ya'."

Margaret packed a burlap bag with biscuits, beef-jerky, coffee, a small pot and two cups. She also filled two canteens with water. It was agreed Bowdie's only chance was for them to get to Tombstone before Frog got to the map. Margaret would wire Piller and tell him to stall as long as possible.

Riley dressed in his clean clothes and good-byes were given. She kissed Riley's cheek than gave Daniel a hug. He and Riley walked to the livery stable and rented two horses ready for travel.

Daniel tied the bag of food to Riley's saddle, adjusted his stirrups, than held the mount while he climbed up into the seat. The horse was tall, and Riley felt as if he were on top of a mountain. He had not done a lot of riding in his life and told his great, great grandfather as much.

Daniel patted his leg, "Don't be worryin' lad, tis' a good ways to Tombstone. By the time we arrive you'll be ridin' like a true cowboy. Of course," he added with a shrug, "you're gonna' be sore." Daniel saw worry in Riley's eyes and grinned, "But ya' needn't be frettin' over a little pain, lad. Ya' got McCaden blood in your veins, and that means you're tougher than most."

Daniel swung up into his own saddle than and they reined south out of town toward Tombstone. Riley glanced at his watch, 2:06am. It seemed like forever since he had had a full nights' sleep. When – if - he got back home, he'd crawl into bed and sleep for three days with a do not disturb sign on the door of his bedroom.

In just a short time the city of Tucson lay well behind, lost to the darkness. The sky looked velvety and the stars brighter than usual; perhaps it was an allusion caused by the openness of the desert. The moonlight mantled everything with silver light.

Riley could see surprisingly well after several minutes. The ground lay spotted with low-set clumps of brush. Giant Saguaro Cactus towered everywhere looking like an army of lost aliens in the moon's glow. The land waved with gentle rolling hills, and a chilling night breeze ruffled their hair. Daniel threw Riley a long-sleeved shirt, "Here ya' go lad. It'll help keep away some of the cold."

Side by side they rode through the night talking. Riley learned a great deal about his great, great grandfather. Daniel's father had been a Druggist too, in Dublin, Ireland, where Daniel grew up learning the trade. He regretted leaving his country, but there had been little work and few could afford the cost of medicine.

From the mouths of young sailors there had come stories of the great America, of its wealth and vast opportunities. The land of milk and honey it had been called, a country of wide open space and unbelievable riches. A country with an explosive love of freedom, a land where a man could choose to be anything he wished and live wherever his heart should lead.

Daniel explained that since his coming here, he had learned to love America too; and that he and Marie would one day return to Ireland to bring back their children, explaining their lives felt empty without them. Riley imagined his own mom and dad feeling the same.

Daniel also told of the hard, labor of love he and Marie shared in building the house in which they now lived; and when Riley told him it was still in the family in 2023, the Irishman smiled proudly.

And so it went. Through the night they talked and laughed, each enjoying the company of the other. The world turned, spinning toward the promise of another day, the promise of a good day. For soon, Bowdie would be back with them again; great grandfather had given his word. And it was the word of a McCaden.

CHAPTER FORTY-TWO

By 7:30 the sun was up, and the desert was warming. Riley was thankful. He had shivered the entire night. The shirt his great, great grandfather had given him helped, but it was by no means a coat.

So the new day grew on. The horses trudged steadily along. The sun grew higher and hotter, beginning to all ready redden their skin.

The leather saddle was doing just as his great, great grandfather had promised; Riley's butt was sore, feeling like the skin had been worn away and every muscle in his butt and thighs were raw and on fire.

Often he thirsted for water but his great, great grandfather restricted his drinking, explaining that their water was limited and had to be carefully preserved. He told Riley that often, when a man crossed the desert, his life depended a great deal on self-control. If he drank every time he wanted, he would quickly run out and begin a slow death from dehydration. Riley understood and never complained.

The repeated movement of the horse grew tiresome. With each step came the relentless bounce followed by the creaking of leather. Riley's legs and rear grew more and more tender, feeling as if they were now beginning to blister. His muscles ached. Living in the wild west was nothing like its portrayal in the movies. Still, each time his great, great grandfather asked how he was doing he forced a smile, and told him fine.

Late in the afternoon the horses splashed across the San Pedro River into a small town called Saint David. It really wasn't much of a place; one main street with a few logged houses, six or seven adobe buildings, a large corral at the far end of main and a small cemetery grown over with weeds. There were Horses tied at three different hitching posts and a handful of people moved busily about.

A small store stood in the middle of town and that's where Daniel reined his horse to a stop. He swung down from the saddle and Riley did the same, grimacing at the pain. Daniel hid his smile.

After tying the animals to the hitching post they brushed dust from their clothes and walked into the store. Riley gave the place a quick glance. It was cluttered. Ceiling to floor shelving had been built on every wall and stacked tightly with all sorts of different things. There were can goods, big bags of flour, sugar and rice. He saw dishes, clothes, buckets, canteens, horse stuff, guns, traps, ammunition, and a lot of other things he had no idea of what they were.

There was a long counter near the door with a big glass bowl on top. It was filled with different colored sticks of candy and Riley was wishing he had a piece. Daniel walked to the counter and stood a moment in silence, looking around. Riley moved to his side.

At first it appeared no one was there but in a few seconds a man came through a back door and spotted them. Making his way behind the counter he smiled. "Sorry. I was out back unloading goods. What can I do for you?"

Daniel looked at Riley. "I'd like the lad outfitted."

"You mean clothes, sir?"

"I." Daniel nodded.

The store keeper came around and measured Riley's waist, leg and arm length, and hat and foot size. Then he began gathering clothes: a light blue shirt, jeans, a buckskin jacket with hanging fringe on the arms, a pair of black boots, a narrow leather belt covered in Indian beads, socks, underwear, and a black cowboy hat to match the boots.

When it was all gathered, Daniel had Riley move behind the counter and put it all on. Then he ordered another outfit of clothes just like those for Bowdie, only for Bowdie he ordered a green shirt.

While Riley dressed, Daniel purchased four more items: three red bandanas and a Bowie Knife. The knife came with a white ivory handle and soft leather sheath with hanging fringe like Riley's jacket.

With the items in hand Daniel walked around the counter to Riley who had just finished changing. "Here ya' go lad." Daniel said as he tied one of the bandannas around his great, great grandson's neck, "In the dessert, dust storms can choke a man till his breathin' stops. When ya' cover your nose and mouth with this, it'll be makin' your breathin' easier. So always keep it with ya'." Because the bandana was red, Riley thought about the Angels of Death Professor Hale had warned them of. Riley said thank you, then his eyes moved to the knife. Daniel McCaden held it out.

"This is for you too, lad. But be rememberin', in the west tis' not a toy. Tis' a man's knife; pulled only when ya' need it; like cuttin' firewood, skinin' an animal for cookin" cleanin' your horses' hoofs, or a weapon if your fightin' for your life. Use it like a plaything and I'll be takin' it away." Riley took the knife. He was honored. "Now, strap it to your belt, Riley McCaden." Daniel said.

Riley nodded and did as told. There was a lump in his throat. He would cherish the knife all of his life…for as long as he lived. And when the day came that he had grown old and ready to die, he'd pass it down to his children, and they'd pass it on down to their children. And so it would become a precious keepsake, a relic of honor, a remnant of a great adventure. Riley promised himself it would remain in the McCaden family forever.

Moving back around the counter, Daniel pulled a small pouch from his pocket. It jingled when he set it on the counter top. A rawhide string held it closed so he opened it up and pulled out four silver dollars. "Here ya' go," he told the store clerk, "This should be coverin' all that we bought."

The clerk nodded, "Yep. That's plenty friend." He then wrapped Bowdie's new clothes and Riley's old stuff in brown paper and tied it with string. "Here you are," the clerk said handing Daniel the package, "you all be careful out there in that desert, a band of Commencharos have been robbing and murdering folks on the trail."

Daniel took the package and nodded. "I, we're grateful for the warnin'." They turned to leave, and the clerk called after them, "Hey son." Riley looked back. "Here," the clerk threw him a long stick of red and white, hard-rock candy. "Enjoy."

Riley caught it and smiled. "Thank you."

On the way out they passed a full-length mirror. Riley stopped to admire his new outfit. He looked like a real, authentic cowboy from the top of his black hat right on down to the heels of his matching boots. The Ivory handle of the Bowie knife looked tall and powerful. He nodded at his reflection. "Riley McCaden," he said to himself with a smile, "Bowdie's waitin', let's ride.

Smiling himself, Daniel walked out the door and Riley followed. And in his heart, a brand-new hope of getting back home raged like a wild fire.

CHAPTER FORTY-THREE

They took time to eat a good meal at the restaurant. Like the store, the place was small with only eight tables. There were no other customers, so they enjoyed a quiet meal with personal service. Riley ordered exactly what his great, great grandfather did: coffee, steak, eggs and fried potatoes with a slice of cake for dessert.

While they ate Riley thanked his great, great grandfather once again for the new clothes and especially the knife with the ivory handle. Daniel asked if he could look at it. Riley proudly pulled it from the sheath and handed it to him. The blade was forward, and Daniel had him turn it around, so the handle came first. "Always lad," he said warmly, "when ya' hand a knife to another, turn it so the handle is toward them. And when ya' take it back, take it gentle."

"Yes sir." Riley said.

Daniel took the knife and turned it over a couple of times in his hands. "Riley," he said after a bit, "do ya' know what kind of knife this is?"

Riley nodded. "It's a Bowie knife, personally designed and made famous by Jim Bowie who died at the Alamo along with Colonel Travis and Davy Crocket in, 1836."

Grinning, Daniel handed the knife back, blade first. Riley raised one of his eye brows, "Great, great grandfather, when handing back a knife it's always handle first. Are you forgetting it's not a toy?"

Daniel smiled wide. "For sure you're a McCaden. Ya' got a sense of humor."

5:30 found them back in the saddle. The land around them was beginning to change. The once rolling hills gradually flattened into wide, open wasteland. Bush clumps grew less and so did the cactus. Here the ground was hard, baked brown by centuries of hot scorching sun. Riley decided he didn't like the desert any more than horseback riding.

By 8:40 dark was nearly upon them so they stopped and made camp. Riley gathered what wood he could find, and Daniel built a small fire. They had ridden upon a small group of Cedar Trees and Daniel constructed the fire in the center beneath thick outstretched limbs. Riley asked why he had built it so close since everything in the desert was dry. It just seemed such an unsafe thing to do.

"Because," Daniel explained, "the trees will be hidin' the flames and the limbs will disperse the smoke. If ya' don't be wantin' trouble, Riley, then don't be sendin' a signal to men who are lookin' for it. That's the rule when ya' travel." Riley suddenly remembered the warning the store owner had given them concerning the Commencharos.

Daniel put over a pot of coffee and in minutes it was boiling. Filling two cups he gave one to Riley. They had removed all gear from the horses and tied them securely to the trees close by. Now leaned against their saddles they relaxed. The fire cast soft shadows across their faces, the stars were out in great numbers and a full moon covered the open desert with its silvery light.

Riley took his first sip of coffee, and it burned his lips. He jerked, and some of it spilled out of the cup, pouring down over his jacket. Quickly he looked to see if his great, great grandfather saw. He had been looking away and Riley was glad. *What a klutz,* he told himself. Moving the cup close to his mouth he began blowing on the hot liquid.

The desert was quiet except for the wind. Feeling he had blown on the coffee long enough, Riley attempted another sip, careful this time. It was still hot but had cooled enough. The black liquid was strong, but that was okay, it was how it should be, after all, they were cowboys camped in the Arizona desert.

Riley took another sip. "Great, great grandfather, do you think the man called Piller will be able to stall Frog long enough?"

Daniel took a sip too. "This man Frog is only a few hours ahead, it'll be takin' him some time to find the man. Ya' can be restin' easy Riley, we'll make it. By noon tomorrow we'll be ridin' into Tombstone, and by nightfall have Bowdie back with us, alive and well."

A piece of fire wood popped, and sparks flew into the darkness. Riley took another sip of his coffee. Back home he would have made a face at even thinking about drinking coffee, more less it being black with no sugar or milk to hide the bitter taste. But here and now it felt natural, and he had to admit it actually tasted pretty good. Maybe he wouldn't sleep tonight because of the caffeine, but leaned against their saddles and sipping a cup of desert made coffee while talking, it all just felt so right.

A sudden burst of wind made the fire flames dance. It was a chilly gust and Riley turned up the collar of his jacket. He was thankful for its warmth and appreciative of the fire as well. But of everything, he was most grateful for the man sitting across from him.

Taking his last swallow Riley yawned. Maybe the caffeine wasn't going to interfere after all. Stretching out he pulled his blanket around him and told his great, great grandfather good night. He laid his head against his saddle. The leather was hard but that was okay, this was the way cowboys slept.

Closing his tired eyes he welcomed the feel of sleep coming. Somewhere in the darkness a lone Coyote howled. Riley's hand slowly slipped down and wrapped around the handle of his knife. Daniel noticed and smiled.

His own coffee had grown cold, so he tossed the remains into the darkness. Stretching out himself he pulled his blanket around him. He too was tired. For several minutes Daniel McCaden listened to the night sounds around him: a piece of firewood popped, and the coyote howled again, one of the horses whinnied and a rush of wind rustled the tree leaves. Satisfied, Daniel closed his eyes. Like his great, great grandson, he too wrapped his hand around a weapon, only his was a revolver.

Through the night they slept. The stars twinkled and the moon cast down its shimmering light. Around them the desert lay quiet as sleep replenished their bodies with new strength and filled their hearts with fresh hope. The wind blew softly, causing fire flames to flicker and red coals to glow. It nibbled at their blankets, howled at the darkness and rolled tumbleweed past their sleeping forms.

Once again Riley dreamed. This time he was home, and it was Thanksgiving. He stood beside his dad at the head of the table with everyone watching. For the first time in his life, he had been given the honor of carving the family Turkey. Proud, he would do a good job, for in his hand he held the big knife with the Ivory handle.

CHAPTER FORTY-FOUR

It was a faint sound that caused Riley to open his eyes. Curled in a ball beneath his blanket he saw light seeping in around the edges. A new day had come, a good day, the day Bowdie was coming back. Sleepily, Riley yawned throwing back the blanket. The yawn ended abruptly. He dared not move.

His great, great grandfather stood only a few feet away surrounded by a dozen Indians with pointed rifles. Riley's mind thought one thing: Commencharos. One of the warriors spotted him and made a motion with the barrel of his rifle, then spoke several words in a language he could not understand. What the Indian wanted, however, was obvious. Slowly Riley rose to his feet and walked to the group. All had turned to watch him approach.

One Indian, obviously the leader, stood directly in front of his great, great grandfather. With nervous eyes Riley studied him. He was a big man, taller than Daniel by several inches. His hair was black like the night and long, hanging loose to his shoulders. A single feather hung from it, held in place by a run of blue beads. His chest was bare and around his left arm he wore a band of beads matching the ones holding the feather. His pants were buckskin and covered at the crotch with a loin cloth. On his feet he wore moccasin boots that laced all the way up to just below the knees. His face was stern and eyes dark.

When Riley entered into the circle and stopped at his great, great grandfather's side, the one with authority turned back to Daniel and spoke. Much to Riley's surprise, it was in English, good English! "So why do you ride through this land?"

Daniel stared back, never blinking. "We are going to Tombstone, to save the life of a young lad."

"Save?" The Indian asked, "If he is in a white man's town, what is it you save him from?"

"The lad has fallen into the hands of an evil man, one who would hurt him for no reason."

"This man is wanted by your law?" The Indian asked.

Daniel shook his head. "No, they do not know about him yet."

The Indian looked thoughtful for a moment, "This man for who you search, does he look like the creature that hops across the ground and croaks from the water's edge when night comes to the earth?"

Daniel threw a look at Riley then answered. "I. That would be him. They call him, Frog."

The Indian turned to his men and spoke in their language. The pointed rifles dropped. He looked back to Daniel. "This man, Frog, we too search for him."

"And why, might I be askin'?" Daniel said.

"A day ago when the sun was high, he killed two of my people at a water hole. One was but a young boy, like this one," he nodded toward Riley, "we thought you might be this man, or his friend."

"No." Daniel told him, "'Tis' only the Devil that would be this man's friend.

The Indian nodded and asked. "When you find him, will you kill him?"

Daniel knew what the Indian wanted to hear but he would not lie, "We seek him only to get back the young lad. I'll be killin' him only if he gives me cause."

The two stared for some time, than the Indian broke the silence. "If this man you call Frog does not die by your hand, when you find him and have the boy back, will you take him to your law?"

Daniel shrugged. "I'd be a likin' too, believe me. But I don't think our law would punish him. We have no way of provin' he's done wrong."

The Indian nodded. "It is truth you have spoken to me. We too have no proof of this wrong doing, only the word of an old woman who he also shot but did not kill. But to the white man, it does not matter, we are Indian and they do not think us human beings. In the white man's world there is no justice for us, we must make our own. For this reason I will ride with you. And when we find this Frog and the boy is in your hands…than I will be this Frog man's law."

Turning, the Indian spoke again to those with him. All mounted and rode away. When they were gone the Indian told Daniel. "I am named Running Horse."

"And I am Daniel. The lad here is called Riley."

Running Horse looked down. "Riley is a good name, it is strong and speaks loud". Riley couldn't help his grin. This was a real 1888 Indian warrior telling him this. In his heart he wished Bowdie could have been there, this was so cool. Running Horse pulled his attention back to Daniel. "Let us ride, I want much to meet the man you call, Frog."

Daniel saddled the horses while Riley buried the fire. When things were packed they rode out. The sun grew hot and blinding, heat waves shimmered across the desert floor. Trees were few so shade was scarce. Sweat soaked their clothing and dust caked their skin.

Step after step the horses ambled on monotonously. Twice, Riley fell asleep in the saddle. In his mind he imagined himself back home in the air-conditioned house, drinking a cold Pepsi and watching a Western movie in his room; where the saddle wouldn't be burning his muscles, the

Sun his skin, and the desert dust and alkali covering his face and clothes. Life was so much easier in 2023.

They rode for some time before anyone spoke; it was the Indian. Pulling up alongside Riley he asked, "So, the boy for who you search, he is your brother?"

Riley shook his head. "Almost, we're best friends."

Running Horse gave a nod. 'It is said among my people that a friend who is true, is worth as much as the food you eat, for without food the body slowly dies. It is the same when you are without a friend, without him, the spirit slowly dies." The Indian's eyes moved to the knife on Riley's side. "That is a good knife."

Riley glanced down at it. "Thank you."

"You are young, why do you carry it?"

Riley pulled his hat from his head, wiped sweat from his brow than replaced the hat. "Well first," he went on, "it's not a toy. I never pull it unless it's necessary. It's used for cleaning my horse's hoofs, skinning an animal for eating, or to defend my life."

Running Horse gave a nod and looked over at Daniel. "You have been teaching your son well, my friend."

Looking at Riley, Daniel winked. "I." he said pulling his eyes to Running Horse, "the lad is growing into a fine young man." Daniel didn't explain how they were really related. In a way, Riley was his son...his great, great son.

CHAPTER FORTY-FIVE

The town of Tombstone was larger than Riley imagined. And much to his surprise, looked a great deal like the movie set used in the filming of the movie, Tombstone, in which Kurt Russel played Wyatt Earp and Val Kilmer Doc Holliday. But this, he grinned, this was the real deal.

There were several streets running parallel to Main with movement on all of them. Unlike the little town of Saint David, Tombstone was busy with riders on horseback and wagons and buggies and people constantly walking and crossing the dirt streets. He couldn't believe all the activity.

Daniel had also warned him the place would be dangerous, filled with gamblers, outlaws and men who had little or no conscious; men who would kill without hesitation or just cause. Riley understood. But it wasn't the outlaws, gamblers or gunfighters of Tombstone, 1888 that worried him. It was the maniac from 2023 that put fear in his heart.

The Crystal Palace Saloon sat on the corner of Main and Third. It was a big two-story building that looked a lot like a Hotel, which in fact it was. It was triangular in shape with four round pillars supporting a front terrace. The bottom floor made up the saloon and the top floor the Hotel.

Riley gave thought to Tombstone's history. Wyatt Erp had been the Marshal here in October of 1882, when he, his brothers and Doc Holliday shot it out with the Clantons at the OK corral. And here he was now,

Riley thought excitedly, in Tombstone only six years following that famous gunfight. Wyatt himself was still young and alive and the OK corral still just the way it was. He wondered if Wyatt would think it strange if he asked for his autograph.

But there was a side to Tombstone that angered Riley too. Running Horse was drawing a lot of stares, most of which were cold and hateful. His Indian friend was a good person; it was obvious people were judging without giving him a chance.

Noticing Riley's irritation Running Horse told him, "Do not let their eyes bother you my young friend. They stare like old women because they fear me. It is because my skin and ways are not like there's. They think me an animal."

"Well it isn't right." Riley snapped. "Someone needs to shake the stupid out of them. Make them realize we're all human beings and equal in our own ways. All of us were made in God's image."

The Indian smiled. "This is so, but who has a voice strong enough to change the minds of as many people as there are leaves on the trees? It angers me as it angers you, but the world is as it is, and will remain so until all have learned to think with the heart as much as the mind. The Great Spirit lives inside all people and cries out for goodness, but only a few listen. You young one, are wise, your ears hear the good words of those who are older, and you learn from them. Perhaps when you have grown, the Great Spirit will use your wisdom to teach others the true importance of the heart."

Riley nodded, "My best friend Bowdie is African American, and he is sometimes called names just because of the color of his skin. And almost always its people who don't even know him."

Running Horse frowned. "I do not understand Riley, what is African American?"

Riley looked surprised. "His skin, its dark. He's black."

"Ah, yes" Running Horse said understanding it now, "I have met good men with skin that dark. Most had been slaves before the white man's war. And as it is with my people, they too are thought to be less than a human being."

Riley nodded recalling 2023. It was a great deal better for both the American Indian and African American in his time. Compared to what he was seeing here, the hearts of people over the years had in fact been changing; waking up. Running Horse had no way of knowing it now, and he had thought little about it himself, but the human heart had been undergoing evolution for decades, incorporating caring, compassion, and acceptance for all races into nearly all decision making. He thought about the President and how far the United States had come. The whole world was in fact becoming a better place, although the idiotic practice of prejudice still remained in far too many hearts.

Daniel reined left and they followed. In front of the telegraph office they dismounted and tied their horses to the hitching post. Riley was still saddle sore, but the pain was easing.

They sent a gram to Professor Hale's sister, informing her of their arrival, then crossed the street and hurried to the Crystal Palace. Riley noted the sound of his boot heels clicking the wooden sidewalk. It was cool, and the jingle of spurs would have made it cooler.

CHAPTER FORTY-SIX

As they drew near the Crystal Palace, a jumble of sounds drifted through the swinging doors: a group of drunken cowboys were singing while trying to stay in time with a piano - they weren't doing so well. There were dozens of conversations using colorful language – words Riley didn't realize were used in those days. Cigar, Cigarette and Pipe smoke floated out in clouds and there was the constant jingle and clanging of whiskey bottles and glasses. It all sounded rough, loud and crowded, but to Riley, it was obvious they were all having a good time.

Daniel stopped just short of the doors. "Riley," he said placing his hands on his shoulders, "tis' best ya' be waitin' here. And you Running Horse," he said looking over at the Indian, "I don't mean to be bruisin' your pride, but I doubt you'd be welcomed either. Best ya' wait here with the lad."

The Indian nodded and Riley did the same. Daniel hadn't even turned when a man come flying through the swinging doors landing in the dirt street. Another stormed out after him and pulled him to his feet. A fight was on. Through the swinging doors there poured a crowd of excited onlookers.

It was a harsh fight. Fist after fist flew savagely. First one man went down, then the other. Chatter amid the crowd was edged with delight, money from bets changed hands faster than the fists of the two men fighting.

Nearly everyone had carried out their beer or whiskey and stood sipping as they watched. When one fighter would knock the other down, cheers would rise. The street was dry, the sun hot, and dust swirled.

Both men were big and burly with one a few inches shorter. Sweat covered them from head to toe. Each blow was hard and powerful. One punch sent the bigger man skirting backward into three horses tied to a hitching post; the animals whinnied and sidestepped but the fight didn't stop.

Passer-byes were joining the crowd. The shorter man took a punch, whirled about and fell to his hands and knees, the other man dived on top of him, and they rolled twice; the crowd cheered. Dust churned in the air.

Suddenly the thunderous roar of a shotgun blast rocked the intensity. The fight stopped and a hush fell over the crowd. A man dressed in a black suit and flat-topped hat calmly approached the two who had been fighting. On the left side of his coat he wore a silver badge that glistened beneath the sunlight. A bushy mustache highlighted his firm, square jaw, and the right barrel of the shotgun cradled in his arms was still smoking. Riley spoke under his breath…Wyatt Earp!

When the Marshall spoke everyone listened. He told the men fighting, "You two get back inside and have another beer," reaching into his pocket he pulled out a coin and tossed it to the tall one, "here it's on me. I come back again you're going to jail."

His attention turned to the crowd. "The rest of you go back to what you were doing, the fights over." With mixed mumbling the bigger part of the mob turned and sauntered back in through the swinging doors, others ambled their way across the street and down the wooden boardwalk. Daniel, Riley, and Running Horse remained.

Looking them over the Marshall approached and spoke directly to Daniel. "Don't reckon I've seen you three around before. Can I help you with something?"

Daniel nodded. "I. Marshall. That you can. We're lookin' for a man. He'd have a young lad with him; a dark skinned lad." Daniel motioned his head toward Riley, "This one's size." The Marshall looked at Riley then back.

"What's your business with this man?"

"He's stolen the lad and will hurt him if we don't get to him quick."

The Marshall shifted the shotgun to the other arm. "How do you know he's in my town?"

"He's come to see a man called, Piller."

For the first time the Marshall's straight face changed; his eyes narrowed. "Piller you say. You mean the barkeep here at the Palace."

"I. Marshall. I was just on my way in to see him when the fightin' broke out."

"Well I'm afraid talking to him is not going to happen. He's not here."

"Is he not workin' then?"

"You might say that. He's over at the undertakers. We found him dead this morning in his room upstairs here. Someone did him in with a knife." Fear for Bowdie turned Riley pale. "Whoever killed old Piller," the Marshall went on, "tore up his room searching for something. You wouldn't have any idea what that something might be, would you?"

Daniel thought a moment, unsure just how much he should tell. Finally, deciding the Marshall had a right to know he told him, "I, we do know, tis' a map he's searchin' for."

"A map you say, a map to what?"

"A map to a whole lot of gold," Daniel paused briefly, "Marshall, would ya' be mindin' if we took a look at that room?"

The Marshall shrugged thoughtfully, "I reckon there's no harm in it. Follow me."

There was a stairway attached to the side of the building leading to the upper floor. Single file they climbed to the top. The Marshall was wearing Spurs and they jingled with each step. Riley grinned with his thought, *yeah, that's what I'm talking about.*

CHAPTER FORTY-SEVEN

The group entered the upstairs. They walked to the center of the hallway and stopped at door number 7. The Marshall turned the handle, and they walked in. The room was small with a single bed, a three-drawer dresser and a well-worn desk and chair. A window over looked the street below; and on the hardwood floor just beneath the sill lay a dark stain. There was no doubt as to where Piller had died.

The Marshall had told the truth about someone searching. The mattress had been sliced open with a knife and its cotton filling lay everywhere. The dresser drawers lay upside down with their contents dumped in a pile. In several places, boards had been ripped up from the floor exposing the wooden joists. If in fact the map had been there, then it was now in Frog's possession.

Daniel stood with his hands on his hips and chewing on his bottom lip. "Well Marshall," he said shaking his head, "Tis' no need for us to be searchin' any farther. If ya' don't mind, we'll be gettin' on our way."

The Marshall gave a nod. "You're free to leave. If you need my help with anything just come by the office and ask for me, Marshall Emmitts." Riley made a face; he wasn't Wyatt Earp.

Emmitts started to leave but paused at the door. "Look" he said, "I don't take to murder in my town. You see this man who you think killed old Piller, you come and get me, hear?"

"I. Marshall" Daniel assured him, "We'll be doin' it. He's a dangerous man." Running Horse was pleased to hear the white man's law was going to make things right.

Leaving the Crystal Palace they walked back to the telegraph office and sent another message to Professor Hale's sister, informing her of the bad news. The wire read:

Sorry. Piller murdered.

Was map in room 7.

Need to know immediately.

Daniel McCaden.

There was nothing they could do now but wait. If room 7 was in fact the place the map had been hidden, then Frog had it and all was lost. But, if it turned out to be somewhere else, then there was still hope.

Hungry, they marched to the restaurant to grab a bite while they waited; but a sign hung beside the door, **'No Ingins and Blacks allowed',"** Angry, Riley wanted to go in and talk with the manager, but Daniel assured him it would do no good. So powerless, they ordered sandwiches instead and returned to the telegraph office.

While they ate, Daniel told Running Horse the story behind the map for which they were searching, explaining it showed the way to the Seven Cities of Cibola, and that Riley and Bowdie needed the map to help them get back home to their own time in history.

Running Horse listened, appearing to believe what he was hearing. When Daniel finished the Indian told them, "Yes, I too know of this Cibola. My people have searched for this place. But we seek it only to protect it from the white man's greed."

Daniel nodded grimly. "I". That is a good thing. And for us, it is only to help the boys."

The wait at the telegraph office felt as if it would never end. But at 3:18pm their reply arrived. Sitting on the steps, they heard the sudden flow of clicking and scrambled inside. The operator was hastily writing down the message. The moment he was finished he passed it to Daniel who read it aloud.

Room 9 Under bed beneath

crooked board.

God be with you.

Margaret

When Daniel finished reading he folded the paper and stuck it in his pocket. After paying the operator, they hurried back to the Crystal Palace. Daniel knocked on the door of room 9, but no one answered. He tried the door, and it was locked.

Glancing quickly up and down the hallway and seeing no one, he forced it open with his shoulder. They slipped inside and closed the door.

The room was occupied by someone. A shirt hung on a hook and several personal items lay on the dresser top. A pair of expensive boots sat in the corner near a rocking chair, and a big leather suitcase sat to the right of the door.

Working together they quietly pushed the bed to the side and found the crooked board just as the telegram said. Kneeling, Daniel asked Riley for his knife and worked the board loose. It took a few minutes but when he pulled it away, there it lay; rolled and tied with a piece of string.

Pulling it free, Daniel rose to his feet and looked excitedly at the others. With nervous fingers he untied it and began pulling it open. It was than the door burst open. Startled, they glanced up. Frog stood there with a gun in his hand, holding Bowdie by the collar. "Okay" he said with a half-smoked cigar between his lips, "hand it over you dim-witted chumps."

CHAPTER FORTY-EIGHT

Realizing Frog had the advantage; Daniel re-rolled the map and tied the string. Frog grinned. "There you go. Now bring it to me you Irish idiot stick."

Riley's jaws tightened and he stepped out from the others. The fat man pulled the gun on him but Riley spoke his mind, "You're the idiot here, you Horses Ass, " Riley realized his words were wrong, but he continued, his anger riling higher, "Your greed and selfishness make you one. You want the map; you come and get it. And you're coming through me first."

Frog stared at Riley with surprise. "Well, well, well." he grinned clenching the cigar tighter, "will you listen to little Danny Junior. How about this instead, first I shoot your best friend then your great, great grampy, and lastly I put a bullet right between the eyes of the Geronimo want-a-be; then me and the map disappear leaving you here all alone with your lonesome."

Daniel stepped between them, placing Riley behind him. "Tis no need to be givin' threats. Here, take it." Daniel said extending his arm.

Frog grabbed the map quickly then using his foot, shoved Bowdie into the room with the others. "Fine." he said, "and in exchange you can have this bag of brown vomit back."

He waved the map saying, "I have one last stop to make, pick me up a few trinkets, worth what, a hundred and fifty million maybe. And remember this, anybody follows me, and it'll be the last thing they ever do."

Looking one more time at Riley and Bowdie Frog grinned, "You know what, you toilet-wipes, I ain't all bad. When I get back I'll drop in and say hello to your parents for you. Let them know you're going to be very late coming home." He pretended to frown, "No wait, you won't ever be going home."

He pulled the door closed while laughing out loud.

Riley looked at Bowdie, "You okay?"

Bowdie sighed, "Yeah. I'm fine now."

Looking up at his great, great grandfather, Riley thanked him. He had kept his word. He had promised to have Bowdie back by dark, and here he stood.

Daniel moved to the door and opened it cautiously, glimpsing out into the hallway. He saw no one. Behind him Running Horse spoke softly. "Do you wish to try and track him my friend?"

Daniel closed the door and stared at the Indian, than pulled his eyes to the boys. They were eager, wanting very much to hunt Frog down. Daniel chewed on his lip considering the situation; there was so much at stake. With Frog in possession of the map the boys were of no particular value to him anymore. That put both of them at high risk. He knew Frog would kill them now just for the fun of it.

Sighing, Daniel ran options through his mind. Renting the boys a room at the Crystal Palace while he and Running Horse alone took up the hunt, was a possibility. But that too had risk. If he himself were killed in the effort, not only would the boys never see 2023 again, but would be stranded here alone in the violent west of 1888. And too, the chances of picking up Frog's trail and staying on it were well against the odds; not to mention the high probability of one or more of them being killed.

Sighing, Daniel made a face. It was a difficult decision. "I'm sorry lads," he said shaking his head, "but the stakes have grown too high. We'll not be chasin' after this madman anymore. Tis' home we'll be goin'." Daniel forced a smile, "but we'll not be givin' up mind ya'. When he shows for the ride back, we'll be waitin' for him."

"Yes," Riley said discouraged, "but he might be expecting that, and even if we over power him, what if he no longer has the map. Or what if something happens to him and he never makes it back?"

Daniel had considered all these possibilities, but the lives of the boys had to come first. His decision was final.

"Wait my friends!"

They turned to look at Running Horse.

The Indian appeared troubled but had something to say. "If," Running Horse began, "I share with you a secret many centuries old; can you keep my words locked away?"

The three glanced at one another, than back nodding in agreement.

"The map you want is gone, but the man called Frog will have it when he reaches the Seven Cities. What if I told you there may be a way we could get there before him."

Daniel was puzzled. "But we do not know where the cities are. And you already said you and your people have been searchin' for them too."

Running Horse agreed, "It is so, we do not know the way to them. But there is a place we can go to seek the answer." The Indian paused. He had more to say, and it was difficult for him.

The room was hot. A bead of sweat streaked its way down Riley's back. Someone walked past the door causing the floor to squeak and the muffled sound of piano music began drifting up through the floor.

"For five generations of my people," Running Horse began again, "there has been kept a secret. Always, even when we were a nation of many, it was the same. The Dancing Spirit, when sought, would sometimes reveal the answer to the greatest of mysteries. We can go to him and ask the way to the place you seek; but to ask will bring great risk for one of you; for to do this, it takes two people, one young and strong, the other old and wise. Each, while in a dream, will be given a clue, and when put together the clues will hold the answer. Unless…" Running Horse quite talking and shook his head. "No, I am wrong to tell you these things, it has too many dangers."

Riley stepped in front of Running Horse. "Please, you have to help us. Risks or not, it's our one and only chance of ever getting back home. I'll beg if I have too."

The Indian looked into Riley's eyes. "Young One, it is an Indian way, never before done with one who is not."

Bowdie moved beside Riley. "Running Horse, the Dancing Spirit you talk about, he's obviously wise, right?"

"He holds the knowledge of all the worlds, yes."

"Well then, don't you think he'll understand how much we need his help?"

Giving Bowdie's words consideration Running Horse slowly smiled. "Like your friend," he said placing a hand on Bowdie's shoulder, "you too are grown beyond your years. I understand why you are friends so strongly. So it will be. We will talk with the Dancing Spirit and ask the way to the Seven Cities."

"All righty than," Bowdie yelled out loud clapping his hands, "Let's do it. What's the modus operandi, we close our eyes, hold hands, kneel, sing, pray, dance…what?"

"Not so fast," the Indian said, "I think modus operandi is to say how do we do it. First, we must ride deep into the desert. It is there we will seek him out."

"Seek him out?" Riley asked, "How?"

"We will gather liquid from the Saquaro, mix it with the leaves of three special plants, then myself and one of you, will drink. We will sleep then, and the Dancing Spirit will come to us in a dream." Running

Horse swallowed, he had more to say and somehow Riley knew it would not be good. "Sometimes the Dancing Spirit chooses to tell quickly, and sometimes he chooses to test those who drink. If the spirit puts us to the test, and we do not pass, then death will come for us and it will be painful. We will not awaken from our dream."

Daniel spoke up immediately, "Running Horse, tis' our problem alone. It'll be me who does the drinkin'."

Running Horse smiled admirably. "No, my friend, it must be me. I know what is to come and I am Indian." His eyes moved to Riley and Bowdie. "But you two must decide who will be the other." Riley looked at Bowdie as Running Horse moved to the door and opened it. "Now come," he said glancing over his shoulder, "time is passing quickly. We must gather that which is needed for our journey."

CHAPTER FORTY-NINE

Daniel had Running Horse wait long enough for Bowdie to change into his western clothes. When dressed he looked into the mirror smiling, "Man, I am one cool double A look alike for Samuel L. Jackson on the set of a Cowboy Movie. Somebody hand me my six-guns."

Running Horse whispered to Riley, "What is double A?"

Riley told him grinning, "It's like a nickname, A.A. It stands for African American."

Then walking over to Bowdie he put a hand on his shoulder and told him, "you know what would really make you cool; a pair jangling of spurs."

Bowdie's eyes narrowed in the mirror, imagining his strolling down the dirt street of Tombstone looking hip with spurs jingling. Quickly he turned to Daniel, "Can we, Mr. McCaden? It would be awesome."

Daniel grinned. "I don't be thinkin' so Bowdie. Not yet anyway."

Leaving the Crystal Palace they lead their horses to the Livery stable. There Daniel purchased an extra mount for Bowdie. When Bowdie swung up into the saddle he smiled once again, saying, "Man, don't you just love that sound; ain't nothin' like the creak of saddle leather?"

Daniel and Running Horse shook their heads. They mounted and all rode off into the desert.

Running Horse stopped three times to pick leaves from different plants. The cactus from which he chose to draw the liquid was tall and oddly shaped. One Limb pointed to the sky and the other toward the ground.

"This," he told them while cutting away, being careful of the sharp spines, "is the cactus of the Dancing Spirit. It gives warning even before we begin. The arm pointing to the sky is a good sign; the promise that the Dancing Spirit will come to hear us. The other is a warning; that once we drink, he will decide our destiny."

Evening seemed quick in coming. Shadows moved steadily across the open land leaving behind a strange darkness. Wind rustled their clothes and swept the desert floor.

When they made camp Daniel removed gear and saddles, than tied the animals securely to the twisted limb of a stubby cedar tree. Riley and Bowdie gathered firewood and Running Horse prepared the secret drink. When the wood was gathered the boys sat and watched the Indian.

He gouged out several small chucks of cactus meat; it resembled pineapple, and they wondered if it would taste as good? Next Running Horse squeezed the juice from the chunks into a clay gourd. When he had about half a cup, he removed the leaves from his leather pouch and tore them into tiny pieces, dropping them into the gourd as well.

By now Daniel had built a fire and was himself watching the strange actions of the Indian. When all the leaves were shredded, Running Horse placed the gourd over the fire and looked up at his friends.

"Now the liquid must boil and the aromas drift to the sky. This will summon the Dancing Spirit." Looking at the boys he said. "It is not too late. Know that once you drink there will be no more chance, and the Dancing Spirit will decide your fate. Has it been decided which of you will drink with me?"

Both boys remained silent turning to stare at one another. Neither wanted to drink, this was no game, and perhaps one of the most difficult decision either would ever have to make. Running Horse remained silent, letting the two think long on the choice. It was Bowdie who brought about a solution. "Why don't we flip a coin?"

Riley agreed and looked at his great, great grandfather. "Will you flip the coin for us?"

Daniel nodded then looked at Bowdie. "Give me your coin lad, the very one that has lead us all here."

Bowdie pulled it from his pocket and placed it in Daniel's hand. Squeezing it tightly, Daniel stared into their eyes. He was chewing on his lip. Without realizing, Riley was doing the same thing. Daniel glanced at Running Horse and the Indian gave a nod. Daniel tossed the coin into the air.

As though mesmerized, all watched it climb. It spun as if rocketing to the stars. Then it stopped, paused briefly, and began its plummet back to earth. Daniel snatched it only inches above the flames. Riley yelled for Bowdie to call it and his best friend shouted heads.

CHAPTER FIFTY

Daniel McCaden' s heart was heavy with questions: first and foremost, would the coin read heads or tails. Would the strange liquid they were about to drink cause pain, was it a hallucinatory drug or some form of poison bordering life or death. Was Running Horse confident he had mixed it correctly? What if it were too strong for a lad as young as Riley or Bowdie? As a druggist, to Daniel these questions were agonizing.

He had grown fond of his great, great grandson; and Bowdie too. The last thing he wanted was for either of them to lose their life. But like it or not this was a risk they had to take. Stretching his hand toward the fire light he opened his palm. All leaned in to see as he raised his eyes and said softly, "Tis' tails."

Bowdie had called heads; he was the loser.

Riley wanted to jump with joy but remained quiet. He was relieved yet unsettled with the turn of fate. Now once again Bowdie's life was on the line. There was silence around the fire. Bowdie looked into each of their eyes as they sat staring back at him; he saw sympathy, concern, and worry, in each of them. It was obvious they cared, and he felt good about it.

Actually, he felt the toss had worked out for the best. Riley had already been through enough because of him. He owed taking this risk for the best friend he had ever had. This was the way it was meant to be.

The remainder of the evening passed with little conversation. Stars lighted the heavens and the gray overcast of a half-moon dimly shadowed the earth. Riley lay on his back chewing on his lip. Hands tucked behind his head he studied the moon. He could see its entire circle, yet only one half was bright and alive: the other lay dark and lonely. It was as if one side of the moon had simply vanished; just the way it would feel if the Dancing Spirit did not allow Bowdie to come back.

Riley sighed shifting his thoughts. His gaze moved to his great, great grandfather. Daniel had made coffee and now sat drinking a cup staring out into the desert. Riley owed him so much: the new clothes for he and Bowdie, their horses and saddles and the Ivory handled Bowie Knife. But mostly he would forever appreciate his help in attempting to retrieve the map and get them back home. All of what he was doing was being done out of love, and Riley dared not think where he and Bowdie would be without him.

Running Horse, sitting in the distant shadows of the fire was chanting softly. Turning unto his side, Riley rested his head in his hand and watched him. They had known this Indian only a short time, yet not only was he willing to share a tribal secret to help them, he was also prepared to risk his own life as well.

Riley realized he was learning a great deal living here in 1888. Sure life was hard: no running water, no fast-food, no flushing toilets, radio, TV and such. But at least if you needed help, your family and friends would stop at nothing to get it for you. And there were other good things too; like no pollution, unsightly factories, and bumper to bumper traffic destroying the Ozone layer, no six o'clock evening news spreading nothing but bad news. 1888, he had to admit, actually offered a whole lot of good things.

Running Horse suddenly stopped chanting and climbed to his feet. Riley pulled himself into a sitting position while watching him move hurriedly to the fire. Sitting beside the flames he spoke with urgency, "Gather quickly my friends. It is time!"

CHAPTER FIFTY-ONE

Running Horse ordered Bowdie to sit beside him. Pulling a long length of Leather-string from his pouch, he had Daniel bind their wrists together. "This," he told Bowdie, "will ensure you and I do not separate during our journey. The place we go is the ancient burial ground of all my people; it is forbidden for those who breathe in this world; but is the center of all knowledge. Many of the creatures in DYROMA, that is the name of where we go, are large and eat the flesh of men. You must be brave and strong, with courage fierce like the great Grizzly. For I tell you my young friend, what waits for us, is like nothing you have ever seen."

"You've been there?" Bowdie asked swallowing hard.

Running Horse gave a nod. "Yes. Many seasons past when I was young like you. I drank with my father to seek the Dancing Spirit."

"See," Bowdie said trying to make the situation better, "it's not that bad, he sent you back."

"Yes," Running Horse said checking the leather binding, "but not my father."

Turning to the fire Running Horse picked up the small gourd of liquid with his free hand. Raising it to the starry sky he began to chant in a tone that rang with worry. The others remained silent, listening to his strange song.

"HI-ah No-mi, Hi-ah-No-mi, Hi-ah-No-mi," The chant lasted for some time. Bowdie couldn't help but feel frightened. He thought it odd that being tied together now, would make a difference later in a dream; reality was reality and dreams were dreams. His heart was beginning to race. He just couldn't believe this was happening…and it was all over a girl.

The wind carried Running Horse's chant out into the open darkness. All wondered what his words meant. The fire flickered and flames snapped against a wind increasing in strength. It felt as though the night was rapidly growing colder; even the stars seemed to be changing, growing distant and dull as the half-moon vanished off and on behind sinister clouds.

Then as if a switch had been struck, the wind stopped, the desert fell silent, nothing moved. Riley looked at his watch. It was exactly midnight! Running Horse stopped his chanting and lowered the gourd. Eyes tense, he looked at everyone, then raised the container to his lips and drank. Everyone held their breath wondering how it would affect him. Nothing seemed to be happening. After several swallows he lowered the gourd slowly and handed it to Bowdie. "Drink quickly, and remember, no matter what, do not leave my side."

Bowdie took the gourd of strange liquid and raised it to his lips. Frantic thoughts raced through his head: land of ancestors, Dancing Spirits, flesh eating creatures, hunting grounds, the seven cities of Cibola, the map, Frog, the time machine, Home!"

Impulsively he drank! Gulping it down and finding its taste bitter. When the gourd was dry, Bowdie took it from his lips and with a shaky hand set it on the ground. Looking at Running Horse he remained silent, his face one of wonder. A pair of frightened eyes asked what was to happen next. To ease his anxiousness Running Horse gave him a warm smile. "Soon, sleep will come for us."

The Indian moved his gaze to Daniel and Riley. "When we sleep, do not try and wake us. No matter what you hear or see, we must not be touched. Only the Dancing Spirit can return us. When he does, if he does, we will wake on our own."

Bowdie could feel his eyes growing heavy, his eyelids began to flutter. Sleepily he glanced over at Running Horse and noticed his eyes were doing the same. Then his ears began to ring, and he heard Running Horse say. "Lay back and let the sleep take us. Our journey begins."

Together they sprawled on their back and closed their eyes, their bound wrists inches apart. Running Horse reached out and took hold of Bowdie's hand, giving it a reassuring squeeze. Sleep was coming like a heavy weight. Bowdie could not move. His eyes were impossible to open, his arms and legs felt like lead pipes. He could feel his breathing begin to slow. Normally it would have scared him, but strangely, he was beginning to feel relaxed and at peace.

Somewhere in his mind he could hear Riley shouting. BREATHE BOWDIE, BREATHE. YOU HAVE TO BREATHE! He pictured Riley frantic and struggling to get to him but his great, great grandfather holding him back. Then the distant voice of his best friend faded away, and Bowdie opened his eyes.

CHAPTER FIFTY-TWO

He was no longer in Arizona. Sill lying on his back he was staring up into the branches of moss covered trees. It was night. Strange noises were coming from the darkness around him, those of animals and insects. But there were other sounds too; ghostly, unearthly cries, like none he had ever heard before. The ground felt wet beneath him.

Through the moss-covered trees he could see the moon. Squinting, he strained for a better look. There were two moons, side by side. Both were giants, perfectly round and the color of blood. They bathed the landscape of this strange world in a dull, red haze. A host of stars hung in the red-blackness and streaks of lightening flashed constantly. Yet there were no threatening clouds, no rain or thunder. The night was calm and warm; no indication of a storm.

Bowdie was freaking. A thick reddish fog covered the ground. It floated around him, over him, up the inside of his jeans, down into his boots, in his ears, up his nose and everywhere else he possessed an opening. It was groping him, nibbling at his skin like the tiny mouths of hungry little fish. Was it attempting to feed on his flesh? Quickly Bowdie pulled himself into a sitting position. The strain from the leather string binding his wrist caused him to remember…RUNNING HORSE!

Turning quickly, he saw the Indian's eyes were closed and he was not moving. All but his face lay buried beneath the Fog.

"Oh dear God, no," Bowdie cried. Frantically he shook Running Horse. "Wake up. Wake up. Please wake up." Running Horse made no response. Panic rushed in, it was overwhelming Bowdie's senses. His voice was laced with fear, "Running Horse you've got to wake up. I don't know what to do."

The Indian remained motionless. The Fear was escalating. Moving swiftly to his knees Bowdie grouped beneath the fog and pulled Running Horse's knife free of its sheath. He would cut the leather string that bound them! But he paused! "YEAH RIGHT!" he said to himself, "THEN WHAT?"

Clutching the knife he tried thinking clearly. Sweat ran into his eyes and he wiped it away.

It was hot here. The air was sticky and there was no breeze. It was like being trapped inside a giant oven filled with plants. What to do? This was a decision someone his age should not have to be making. Yet he had no choice. There was no one else; Running Horse was…dead! Now he was alone in the land of Dyroma where wild beasts hunt down people and eat them, and worse, he had no idea how to get back.

Bowdie realized his hands were shaking. His entire body was shaking. That's when he realized it was the ground trembling beneath him. *Just freaking great!* He thought. *An earthquake!*

His thoughts ran rampant. What if the very ground he was kneeling on suddenly split open; pulled apart and swallowed him? How far would he fall into the earth…wait, this wasn't the earth, so anything could be down there. "Put a sock in it, Bowdie," he screamed at himself, *"Be cool! Think! You got to think! Okay, here it is. Cut yourself loose from Running Horse and get away to a safe place. This fog is probably an acid and already beginning to eat away the top layer of your skin. You have to get out of it.*

Once again Bowdie moved the knife to the leather string. He started to cut but stopped. Running Horse's words came flashing back, **'No matter what, do not leave my side'.** Bowdie wiped away sweat again and spoke into the darkness, "Man, what the Hel-o-copter am I supposed to do?" He looked at Running Horse's motionless form, "surely you didn't mean not leave your side if you were DEAD." The fog had now nearly covered the Indian's face. Right or wrong, something had to be done, and fast. The ground around him was shaking worse.

Bowdie caught his breath. It was a sudden realization that caused his eyes to narrow. For the first time he noticed the noises around him had stopped as if every creature and insect had run for its life. But to where; and from what, an earth quake?

"That's it," he said, "I'm cutting it." He pulled the knife back to the binding and barely touched the leather when the twin moons suddenly dimmed, darkening the area around him. In the same instant the trembling ground fell still. Bowdie didn't move. Nothing stirred. Holding his breath, careful not to move to quickly, he lifted his face and looked up into the dark sky.

There, towering above the tree tops nearly blocking both moons stood a creature, a beast of unimaginable size. Its shape was frightful. It was not a Dinosaur, not a giant insect, nor was it some mystical Dragon with tucked wings and mouth of fire.

This was definitely something else. And whatever it was, it was staring down into the trees, obviously searching for movement. Seeing none, it raised its head and screamed into the night, the sound terrifyingly loud. Bowdie knew what it was doing; the creature was hungry. It was hoping to scare something into running.

CHAPTER FIFTY-THREE

Bowdie remained motionless, staring up at it, his body electrified with fear. A scream of his own was welling up inside like an inevitable time bomb. His mind told him **No, don't scream, it will hear…that's what it wants.** But he couldn't help it. There was no overriding the terror.

From the bottom of his lungs the rising scream rose like a rush of wind speeding through his throat. Wider and wider his lips parted to let it out; then a hand clamped over his mouth. "Yell out now my young friend," Running Horse whispered, "and neither you nor I will live long enough to hear the end of your scream."

Bowdie nodded silently behind the strong hand and Running Horse released his grip. Bowdie glanced at the Indian with thankful eyes, then back to the monster towering above the trees. Its body was massive, shaped like a man, muscular, but covered in scales. Its head, however, was far from human; it was like that of a serpent, a snake with slanted eyes diamond shaped and yellow. It blinked constantly and a long narrowed forked tongue slithered in and out of its mouth. This thing towered and weighed tons.

For a time it stood its ground, twisting its snake-like head this way and that; staring through the trees below, repeatedly sniffing the air. Bowdie feared it would smell them.

He and Running Horse had awakened in a small clump of trees surrounded by open fields. Had they not been in the trees, the creature would have undoubtedly spotted them long ago. Bowdie wondered if their good fortune had been through the help of the Dancing Spirit.

The small island of trees did provide some cover, but not enough. Beyond the fields lay a dark forest. Bowdie hated to even imagine what might be living in there, but at least they'd have plenty of cover.

Motioning toward it, he whispered to Running Horse, "Should we make a run for it?" The Indian shook his head, "Too dangerous. The creature would catch us long before we reached its edge."

Giving it thought Bowdie agreed. To the towering monster the trees were little more than thick brush. On the run across the open field their moving forms would be easy prey, visible, and the creature would make it a game of Monster Cat and human mice.

Several long minutes passed. Bowdie grew fidgety. The strange fog continued to nibble at his skin and the heat grew intense. He had begun sweating profusely and feared more than ever the snake-man would sense their presence. However, the wait ended. As suddenly as it appeared, the giant moved on. Once again the ground beneath them trembled and light from the twin moons returned. And although slowly, so did the strange noises of the things they could not see.

Bowdie handed Running Horse his knife, "Man, you have no idea how happy I am right now. I thought you were dead!"

The Indian grinned. "Remember my friend. I too was here as a young boy. I know what it is you feel." Running Horse climbed to his feet, pulling Bowdie up with him. He placed the knife back in its sheath. "Come, we must move quickly into the forest."

Still bound they ran swiftly across the open land and into the edge of the woods. Here light from the two moons greatly diminished, but after several minutes their eyes adjusted and the area became surprisingly illuminated.

The forest floor was thick with Fern nearly as tall as Bowdie. And they were a strange plant life, with leaves as large as elephant ears and covered with what felt like a thick film of human hair. Their very touch gave Bowdie the creeps.

"Is it here in the forest we meet with the Dancing Spirit?", Bowdie asked as they moved.

"No," Running Horse told him, "we go to the mountains of the spirits. There we will find the burial ground. And in the center of it we will build a fire and wait. Out of the flames the Dancing Spirit will rise."

"When he comes, will he sit and pow-wow with us?" Bowdie asked.

Running Horse frowned, "What is pow-wow?"

Bowdie made a puzzled expression. "You know, sit Indian style on the ground, smoke the peace-pipe and talk philosophically?"

Running Horse pressed his lips thoughtfully, "He will speak with us yes, and give us riddles. But I do not think we will smoke."

They pushed deeper into the Forest with Bowdie on the verge of pouting. *Man, I can't believe we're not going to pow-wow. That is so cool in the cowboy movies.*

CHAPTER FIFTY-FOUR

In the night sky the strange whips of lightening continued, allowing second-long glimpses of this bazaar frightful world; it chilled Bowdie to the bones. He found himself wishing he were a United States Marine. He'd be dressed in camouflage, face painted and armed with an automatic assault rifle. And he'd be carrying grenades, a survival knife, pistol, food, water, matches, tent, sleeping bag and flashlight with extra batteries. He'd turn himself into Samuel L. Jackson and change his name to Big Bad Black Dude; then things would be different. He'd push through this weird crazy Forest with one outlook…*yeah baby, bring it on.*

The air inside the forest remained hot and sticky, sweat saturated their clothing. At one point they had stirred up a nest of sleeping mosquitoes. The insects were the size of Bowdie's hand with stickers the length of sewing needles. The two had run frantically, swatting and yelling while dashing through the hairy fern. Their massive numbers created the buzz of a chainsaw. Neither Bowdie nor Running Horse were bitten, but both had run themselves into near-fatigue by the time the hungry pack gave up and returned to their nests.

The dark forest was always the same, filled with sounds that triggered their imagination: the snapping of twigs, huge things fleeing the trees with flapping wings, the eerie cries of strange animals and oddest of all, the frequent distant yell of what sounded like human voices crying out in a language totally unknown.

For the most part their movements were slow and taken with careful watchful steps. The going was tiresome and nearly two hours passed before they stopped to rest. The place they chose was a small circular clearing where a large fallen tree lay across its center. Here there were no ferns and a comfortable, thick grass covered the ground. The clearing opened to the heavens and the red moonlight beamed down as if where a giant spotlight.

Thankful for the time-out Bowdie plopped down at the fallen tree. Exhausted, he leaned back and closed his eyes. He thought about home. The first thing he'd do the day he got back would be raid the refrigerator, than take a long hot shower. After that he'd sleep, wake up, go to the bathroom, sleep some more, wake up, go to the bathroom, and eat again, than go back to sleep and finally wake up with life back to normal.

Thoughts ran endless through his mind with visions of family and friends and school. Not realizing, Bowdie slowly fall into a restful sleep. He slept for some time and it was a soft bright light that woke him. Sunshine! Morning had come.

A golden brilliance swept over the Forest and now he could see clearly. The light was warm on his face. Everything looked different in day light. Clumps of gray moss hung from all the trees, and everywhere vines like those found in South American Jungles dangled to the Forest floor - all except the vines hanging within the clearing.

These were a species all their own, entwined with a network of similar vines networking through the treetops. Bowdie also noted they were narrower and clear in color, almost Transparent, and were all somehow fastened to the grass, as if interwoven. He had never seen anything like it and gave them a name, the *Albino Vines of Freak Land*.

Although the dead tree which he leaned against possessed none, Bowdie also observed some form of ivy plant wound its way around and up the trunk of every tree in the forest, climbing high into the branches. The plant's leaves were small and the purist of white. Huge black thorns covered the vine's body as if serving as protective armor; and those thorns Riley saw, moved slightly every few seconds clicking against one another;

as if a noise serving as a warning for all to stay away. It was creepy, and Bowdie shook his head. The entire forest looked as though it had been designed by the imaginative minds of the Walt Disney World theme-park creators.

Suddenly above his head a giant shadow darkened the sky. Quickly Bowdie glanced up. A bird the size of a small aircraft had sailed past but was gone in seconds. Was this another helping hand from the Dancing Spirit?

It took little thought to realize that, had he been running through the open field just now, the winged creature would have easily swooped down, buried its claws into his shoulders and carried him away like a small rabbit.

Unable to stop the thought, Bowdie imagined his being flown above a nest of giant baby birds and dropped. He pictured himself tumbling through the air and crashing into the middle of its Nest; then his body savagely ripped apart by the starving, giant beaks of Baby-Bird Monsters. Bowdie's face twisted into a disgusted expression; *it was idiotic thinking like that, then again, did it matter, he was probably going to die right here in weird land anyway...so what the heck, he may as well mellow...after all, how often is it one gets to dream in psychedelic world with an Indian Warrior and giant Monsters who eat human flesh; a trip of trips, all while high on Arizona Cactus Juice.*

Bowdie closed his eyes and shook his head. *He didn't know if he wanted to laugh or cry.*

Running Horse had been sitting crossed legged, praying softly. He now rose to his feet, "Come, we must move on."

Bowdie attempted to get up but couldn't move. Something was holding him against the fallen tree. Trying harder, he struggled again but it was no use. He yelled to Running Horse. "I can't get up, I'm stuck."

The Indian moved quickly to his side and knelled. He leaned Bowdie forward as much as possible and looked behind him. In the same instant a movement caught Bowdie's eye. At the far end of the clearing something was charging through the tall fern, he could see the tops of the plants waving. Whatever it was, it was moving fast and heading straight for them. Then his eyes caught another movement. Something dark and large was scurrying down one of the transparent vines. Bowdie began to panic, "What the freaking crap Running Horse, Something Is Coming!"

CHAPTER FIFTY-FIVE

Running Horse pulled back and looked at Bowdie. "Coming? Coming where?"

Now Bowdie was screaming. "On the other side of the clearing, moving through the ferns straight toward us, and now something is coming down the vine over there."

Running Horse glanced over his shoulder, looked in the direction of the ferns and then the vine. Turning back he mumbled something in his own language and hurriedly pulled his knife from its sheath. "We must get away quickly, I know what holds you."

Bowdie's eyes opened wide looking at Running Horse,. "WHAT?"

Wildly Running Horse worked the knife behind Bowdie's back, cutting away at something. Bowdie asked again, his eyes moving back to the wild waving ferns, "DEAR GOD, WHAT'S HOLDING ME? WHAT'S COMING?"

Running Horse remained too focused on what he was doing to answer. Three more of the dark things had joined the others and were now scurrying down different vines. They dropped onto the grass, scurried toward them and came into view. Bowdie screamed the word… "SPIDERS!"

And they weren't ordinary spiders. These were huge multi-legged creatures, black as night and the size of footballs. Their pinchers looked like cow horns. Now, like Running Horse, Bowdie knew what it was that held him; it was webbing. Like a trapped fly, there was no escape, and these creatures had one primitive thought on their minds; kill and eat.

The scurrying insects realized their trapped food was fighting hard to get free, so they began to run. Bowdie panicked, wiggling frantically to break free from the web's glue-like hold. The movements made it difficult for Running Horse's efforts, so he yelled "Do not move, I am almost finished."

The oversized spiders were but a few feet away now. Bowdie could see them clearly. An army of nine raced toward them, their hairy legs scampering frantically.

They were ugly things. Huge dark eyes stared out from glossy hair covered bodies. The giant pincers protruding from their mouths dripped with hunger crazed saliva and they squealed with determination.

Running Horse made the last cut and pulled Bowdie to his feet yelling at the same time, "Run. We must reach the trees and charge through the Fern. They will follow only a short distance."

The Spiders were dangerously close, nearly touching their heels and madly snapping their pincers. Their squealing had grown loud with angry. The trees outside the clearing looked a mile away. Bowdie cried out, "We're not going to make it!"

"We will make it," Running Horse shouted, "just run fast and do not fall."

They crashed into the thick fern with great force. The huge leaves slapped at their bodies with some ripping free and twirling into the air. Side by side they dodged trees and hurtled fallen limbs, and never once did they turn to see behind them. Deeper and deeper into the strange forest they plunged, running as fast as humanly possible, until finally, after putting nearly a mile between them and the band of pursuing insects, they slowed to a gradual stop.

Bending, they fought to catch their breath. Their breathing was harsh, coming in wheezes and rasps, their hearts were pounding. The creatures, just as Running Horse said, had at some point given up. Glancing at Bowdie the Indian smiled, "You see, did I not say we would make it?"

Still bent with hands resting on his knees, Bowdie looked at him, "I didn't mean to doubt you Running Horse, but those things looked a lot bigger to me than they did you."

The Indian laughed. "Yes, my young friend," he said, "of that there is no doubt. They would have eaten me first and saved you for dessert."

CHAPTER FIFTY-SIX

By late afternoon they had reached the far end of the Forest and spotted the mountains for which they searched. "How far away are we?" Bowdie asked.

Running Horse studied the distance. "It is several miles, three maybe. We will be there before night darkens our way.

Leaving the Forest they crossed another open field stretching a mile or more. By the time they reached the mountains base, climbed to its top and stood staring into the forbidden burial ground, less than an hour of daylight remained.

Bowdie looked on with wonder. It was nothing like he expected. The dead did not lay on elevated platforms as found in Indian lore, and there were no mounds where graves should be; instead, for as far as he could see, human and animal skeletons lay on top of the ground, exposed. There numbers were mind-boggling.

The majority of remains appeared whole and complete, but some lay with bones missing; probably carried away by animals scavenging for food.

Before they entered, Running Horse and Bowdie gathered an arm full of wood for their fire. The burial ground itself lay flat, bare and open, covered only with the skeletal remains.

The moment the wood was gathered, Running Horse pulled Bowdie hastily along, maneuvering cautiously through the grounds, but just under twenty minutes he ended the force march saying, "This is the place."

Bowdie glanced about. It all looked the same with skeletal remains stretching off in all directions. "Are you sure?" He asked. "How do you know?"

Kneeling, pulling Bowdie down with him, Running Horse laid a hand on the skull of a skeleton lying at his feet. Around the neck of the remains lay a necklace of Bear Claws. "We are in the right place," the Indian said quietly, "the skeleton I touch is my father. The necklace he wears bears his name, Claws of the Bear. It was here I saw him for the last time."

Bowdie glanced at Running Horse. The Indian's eyes were filling with tears as he stared warmly at the remains. He was grieving, remembering; bearing the pain that comes with reliving a bitter-sweet memory. Bowdie understood; it was here as a young boy Running Horse had seen his father for the last time. And now through strange mystical means they had been reunited. Sadly however, all that remained of his father were bones.

Running Horse stood abruptly, "Come," he said, "we must build our fire away from my Father. I have touched him and made the ground where he lies, unclean."

Forty feet to the south they found a spot open enough for their ceremony. Once Running Horse had the fire going, he returned to his father's remains and knelled, once again pulling Bowdie down with him. Clutching the necklace he cut the leather holding it and returned to the fire with it in his hand. There he removed one of its claws, touched it to his lips then tossed it into the flames. Bowdie jumped when the fire flared dramatically.

Running Horse lifted his face to the night sky and shouted several words in his own language, then lowered his eyes and began to chant and dance, circling the fire. Bowdie was pulled helpless behind.

Around them the strange graveyard lay silent. Heard only were the rattle of claws and rhythm of the chant. The night air lingered, feeling stagnant and hot. Their faces glistened with sweat. And eerily, the firelight created shadows that danced beside them.

CHAPTER FIFTY-SEVEN

Running Horse's ceremony lasted for some time. Twice Bowdie nearly stumbled. The twin moons had returned and draped the endless sea of bones the color of red; and with each flash of the strange lightening they glistened as if painted in blood. Bowdie couldn't be sure, but he would have sworn in between flashes the skeletons were changing positions.

Running Horse suddenly stopped and Bowdie went crashing into him. Ignoring it, the Indian lowered himself into a sitting position and Bowdie followed. "I have summoned him," Running Horse said glancing at Bowdie, "Now we wait."

Eyes fixed on the flames Bowdie wondered about the Dancing Spirit. What would he look like: a ghost, a skeleton like all the others, an Angel of beauty? Or perhaps a Demon with pin- pointed ears and razor-sharp teeth?

And what if, Bowdie thought with a shutter, the Dancing Spirit decided to not let him return? His brown eyes widened recalling all the strange things that had already happened since their arrival here, like the snake man. No doubt there were lots more freaky things out there. And how would he eat? Or worse, how would he keep from getting eaten!

Suddenly something out in the darkness screamed. Bowdie jumped yelling a four letter word that would have gotten his mouth washed out with soap had he been home. The fire flared at the same instant but quickly quieted. Snapping his head Bowdie looked at Running Horse for explanation. He never got one. Out of the darkness came a new sound: footsteps and they were moving directly toward them.

Again Bowdie's eyes widened. This was it; they were about to meet the Dancing Spirit. Nervously he drummed his fingers against his knees. The footsteps grew louder. Bowdie's drumming grew stronger. Then like an explosion the spiritual scholar stepped out of the darkness and into the light.

Bowdie's brow wrinkled. He glanced quickly at Running Horse then back. The great, all knowing, ever powerful Dancing Spirit was an ordinary Indian: bare chest, buckskin pants, beaded moccasins, long black hair holding a single feather, and he was no older than Running Horse.

Suddenly Bowdie felt himself being pulled to his feet as Running Horse stood. Across the fire the spirit stopped and stared at them in silence.

Lightening flashed and the graveyard of skeletons glistened with red, then darkness hid them again.

It was Running Horse who broke the silence. It was but a whisper, "Father!"

CHAPTER FIFTY-EIGHT

Running Horse and his father embraced. For some time they held one another, saying nothing. What a cool thing, Bowdie thought, Running Horse seeing his father after all those years, after losing him here so long ago in this strange land.

When the two separated they sat crossed legged on opposite sides of the fire. Running Horse began. "Father, this is Bowdie Pager, he has done well on this journey."

Running Horses' father gave a curt nod. "I am called Claws of the Bear. The journey you take here, I have taken it with my father, and again with my son, who sits here now with you. I know well what you feel." He glanced at Running Horse, then again to Bowdie, "Be proud you are hear, few get to come. It is an honor. And know too, if you are a friend to my son, Running Horse, then forever you shall be a friend to me." Turning to Running Horse then, he spoke with urgency.

"My son, the Dancing Spirit has allowed me to come to you in his place. He knows the reason you are here and understands. But I have been told to say the seven cities are forbidden, you may not enter them. He has granted you riddles. If you solve them you will learn the way, but again I give warning, you cannot enter beyond their gates."

Running Horse nodded with concern, "Yes father, but we must have the map, for without it Bowdie and Riley will not be able to return home to their own time in history. What if it happens we must enter into the city to recover the map?"

Claws of the Bear listened intently, nodding his understanding. "You must all have faith my son," he said, "for if the boys are to return home, it will be their faith that makes it so."

Claws of the Bear fell silent than and stared a few moments into the fire. He was searching for the words he wished to say. After studying the flames for a short time he turned back to his son, "When you and I came here together, when you were young, I lacked this faith and so have remained here to learn and remind others who come here of its importance. I have it now and in turn give it to you. The Dancing Spirit knows all, both good and bad. He sees the future path of all who live and walk upon the earth."

Bowdie spoke up quickly. "Claws of the Bear, does he know if Riley and I will get back home?"

The Indian looked mindful into Bowdie's eyes. "Be careful of the things for which you seek an answer. Sometimes knowing what will happen can change that which should have been."

A soft wind began to blow suddenly, and Claws of the Bear turned his eyes once more to his son. "I must give you the riddles of the Seven Cities quickly, for my time with you is soon gone." He spread out his arms in gesture. "Around you lay the bones of our people, those who sleep. We see them with our eyes. We know they are there. But the bones of the sleeping white man are invisible. Yet we know they too are there. So it is with the Seven Cities."

Claws of the Bear pulled a small stone from a leather pouch tied to his side. The wind was growing stronger. Claws of the Bear spoke hurriedly to Bowdie. "This is a single stone Young Bowdie. The white man's faith is built upon s single stone. Near the forest of the Saguaro stands a great lodge built upon such a stone. There lies the doorway."

Claws of the Bear climbed to his feet and Running Horse and Bowdie followed. Claws of the Bear looked at Running Horse, "Give to me the necklace, my son." When Running Horse handed it to him, his father removed one of its Claws and smiled. Then he handed it to Bowdie "This is for you" he said, "a reminder of your journey here. There will not be many who will believe your story when you tell it, but the claw will forever keep it alive in your heart."

The wind suddenly blow with a howling gust and Claws of the Bear turned to his son, "Hurry, and sit. It is time for you to leave this place. When I am gone lie back and close your eyes.

From the flames the Spirit will rise and send you back. You must keep your eyes closed and for no reason look upon him."

Claws of the Bear looked at his son one last time, wetness filled his eyes. He wanted to give his son one last embrace and Running Horse too craved the same for his father. But there was no time. Slowly Claws of the Bear moved back into the shadows and disappeared.

CHAPTER FIFTY-NINE

Running Horse quickly stretched out on his back pulling Bowdie down with him. Following a quick glance at one another they closed their eyes. The wind grew into a savage gale, howling and blowing with madness. And mixing within its thunderous roar arose yet another clamorous sound; the resemblance of a thousand clanging wind chimes. Bowdie shouted into the deafening racket, "What's happening Running Horse?"

The Indian yelled his warning. "You will see when your sleep comes, but do not open your eyes until the spirit tells you. Do not so much as steal a glance."

Bowdie understood. He held his eyes closed tight and within seconds felt his eyelids growing heavy. Once again his arms and legs felt weighty as if filling with lead. Sleep was coming and his breathing grew shallow. A feeling of peace and joy fell over them both and sounds faded into silence. Then out of the darkness came a shout… "Awaken."

Both opened their eyes and immediately their bodies began lifting from the ground, floating upward still in the lying position. The wind returned, howling and swirling, pushing fiercely against them. Bowdie looked to Running Horse shouting above the noise, "are we going to die?"

"Do not worry my young friend" Running Horse shouted back, "they are only preparing to say goodbye."

"Who is?" Bowdie shouted.

"My people. Their Heaven is returning."

Higher and higher the bodies of Running Horse and Bowdie lifted, until suddenly their positions shifted, and they were turned upright as if standing, now able to observe all that was happening below. Suspended, held by nothing visible they hung in the sky. Bowdie was filled with both amazement and fear as he watched below; witness to something no living person had ever seen.

As if caught in the eye of a tornado, an endless sea of bones swirled in high speed frenzy. Spinning round and around, tumbling and clattering, colliding again and again, searching, seeking the body to which they belonged. It was a massive puzzle of human and animal bones in quest for the reconstruction of the body that once was, all clicking and snapping perfectly into place when located.

Thousands of completed skeletons were now standing upright. And at a speed almost invisible to the eye, Bowdie watched a metamorphosis only God Himself could perform: on each of the skeletons trillions of cells formed, growing and expanding, creating veins and arteries, organs, muscle and skin... all of it networking and connecting at microscopic speeds; shaping, restructuring, giving life back to the body that once was. And upon completion of their flesh and blood rebirth, clothes and hair formed, weaving and entwining, covering them the way they looked before death brought them to this strange place.

Suspended there, weightless, held by supernatural means, Bowdie and Running Horse watched it all in wonder. And when the final skeleton had at last been reborn, the astonishing transformation ended and a new one began...

The wind stopped and a hushed calm followed. Out of the darkness arose a dazzling sun. And as its golden light devoured the blackness, it gave birth to a new world of awesome colors. Once again at speeds the human eye could not follow, meadows and valleys, mountains and rivers and lakes formed. The sky turned blue and the purest of white clouds filled its endless expanse.

The once forbidden world was transforming into a paradise of Indian people: men, women and children; thousands, hundreds of thousands, all returned to a time when the joy of peace and love for a land created by the hand of God was a Heaven on earth.

And when it finally ended, an unblemished world of inconceivable beauty lay stretched before their eyes. Bowdie and Running Horse looked upon it unable to speak, a special joy dancing in their soul. Everyone below was now looking up at them. All were smiling and waving good-by. And amid their great numbers, roaming and grazing and scurrying about at play, were Buffalo and Dear and Bear and every other kind of animal ever known to the Indian people.

Breaking into a smile himself, Bowdie raised his hand and waved back. This new world was perfect, one of peace and love and only happiness. He yearned to be down there with them, wanted to stay. Then his eyes opened.

Around him it was quiet and dark; he lay on his back. Running Horse lay beside him. They were still bound. The fire was burning, flickering softly, the night sky was filled with stars, and a full moon sat hovering over the earth. Then he turned and saw Riley sitting beside him, and Daniel too. They were back!

Bowdie quickly pulled himself into a sitting position this time pulling Running Horse up with him. "Man, Riley," he said with enthusiasm, "you should have been there. That place was the perfect balance between crap and freight and cool and God.

CHAPTER SIXTY

Running Horse pulled his knife and cut the leather binding them. "No longer do we need to be tied my friend," he said, "our journey is over. You were brave and did well."

Realizing the others were curious about what had happened, Horse and Bowdie sat around the fire telling of their experiences in the land of DYTOMA. They described all the wondrous things seen and experienced. Riley and Daniel grew envious, wishing it had been them that had gone.

The talk lasted just under an hour and as they chatted, Daniel cooked a scrawny rabbit he'd shot. Running Horse and Bowdie discovered their adventure had created an appetite big as the snake- man.

While eating they turned to the problem at hand. First, they discussed the riddle given to Running Horse by his father. Claws of the Bear had talked about the graveyard of his people, pointing out that their bones were visible while the bones in the white man's graveyard were not. And that such was the way to the Seven Cities.

Daniel thought a moment and was first to speak, "The answer must be in comparin' the two graveyards."

"Yeah," Riley said chewing on his lip, "At the graveyard in Dyroma, the bones were all lying on top of the ground in the open. Here they are buried in caskets. Maybe it has something to do with being in a confined space."

"Or maybe it has something to do with headstones". Bowdie injected. "There were no headstones at the Indian burial ground, but there are at ours. Maybe at the cemetery near Tucson, there's some kind of clue written on a headstone, someone whose last name is Stone or something."

"No. I think it is something else." Running Horse said.

There was silence for a time. Daniel threw another piece of wood on the fire, and it flared up for a second. When it did another idea struck him. "In your graveyard Running Horse, the bodies were on top of the ground. Here they are underneath the ground. Maybe..."

Running Horse quickly interjected. "Yes. That is it, Daniel. You have found the answer. The riddle tells us the Seven Cities lie under the earth. They cannot be seen, but they are there. Just like the white man's dead."

Everyone agreed excitedly. Now they focused on the other half.

They turned to Bowdie. He thought a few moments recalling what he'd been told. "Claws of the Bear said my faith was built on a stone. He said near the Saguaro Forest there was a lodge built on a stone, a lodge of course meaning a house. He said this place would hold the doorway."

Running Horse frowned, "Near the Saguaro Forest in the White man's city of Tucson there are many lodges built of stone. But they are far too many to search, and too little time to do so."

Riley blurted it out, "JESUS!" Everyone turned. "He was talking about Jesus." Riley said, "That's it, Claws of the Bear was talking about the Savior. Jesus is called the corner stone of the Christian faith."

All four yelled it together... "A CHURCH!"

Eagerly Running Horse told them, "Yes. Very close to the Saguaro Forest stands a Spanish Mission. It is called the Mission San Xavier del Bac. That my friends, is the place we seek." He looked into each of their faces. "It is there, in the house of your God, beneath the floor we will find the Seven Cities."

CHAPTER SIXTY-ONE

They rode out at sun up. Gray stretched clouds were flushed red by the tip of the rising sun. The horses, like themselves, were rested and eager. The morning air was cool, but they paid little attention. This ride would be the ticket to get them home.

It was a three-hour ride to the Mission. With luck Frog would not get there before them. If he did, and he entered the cities to plunder and had the map in his possession, all would be lost. The Angels of Death would never let him leave. And they themselves could not enter beyond the gates to retrieve the map.

They rode hard not stopping to rest. Only twelve days remained before the TT-V returned. It was crucial they take possession of the map and get back to Lafayette. When the machine took off this time, the boys would have to be on board; if not, then they would remain here in the past forever.

It was 10:12 am when they got their first sight of San Xavier del Bac. The place was beautiful. Of Spanish design, it was constructed of stone and adobe with two giant bell towers, one on each side of the main entrance. There were balconies and windows and doors everywhere.

Running Horse had said it was built in 1797, and over the years had converted many of his people into the White man's religion. At the front gate they dismounted, tied the horses to the hitching post and talked for a few minutes before entering. Running Horse had warned of letting the monks know the true reason for their being there. So it was decided they would ask for a place to rest and request permission to take a tour. During that tour they would look for a way beneath the floors.

An old monk in a tattered robe came out to greet them and they explained their need for rest. Warmly he invited them in. The interior was astonishing. Beautiful wood statues of saints, the Virgin Mary and of Jesus stood in alcoves hollowed into the walls. Everywhere huge paintings hung high and low, and hand painted murals decorated the ceilings. Bowdie remarked it was like being inside a museum.

The old man led them to a kitchen where he began preparing their food. Daniel inquired about a man who sounded like a Frog when he talked, and was told no such person had been seen. He then asked how long it would be before the food was ready. When the old monk said twenty minutes, Daniel asked if they could walk around and look at the paintings and murals. The monk agreed with no hesitation.

Out of sight, they quickly searched for a way into the basement. Bowdie was the one who found it. In a small room behind the Alter, a thick wooden door stood draped behind a set of long, thick curtains made of crushed red velvet. Three dust covered chains with huge locks held the door shut. Obviously it was intended no one was ever to enter.

Using their knives, Running Horse and Riley worked lose the old hasps beneath the locks. Daniel and Bowdie kept a nervous look out. When the last chain fell free they tried the door, but it wouldn't budge; scaled by centuries of not having been opened. All grew anxious. Time was running out, the old monk would soon have their food ready and come looking.

Utilizing their knives once again, they dug out the dirt packed in the cracks and around the hinges, than tried again. All four pulled, groaning, teeth gritted, and it gave way this time, swinging outward throwing up a large haze of dust.

Huddling together they peered inside. There was a small foyer with a wood platform and stairway descending down into a pitch-black darkness. The entire foyer was thick with cobwebs.

Running Horse quickly retrieved a candelabra and handful of matches from the Alter. When back, he lit the candles then poked the light through the cobwebs. The entrance way lit up. The timbers used to construct the old foyer and stairway stood warped and stooping, much of it rotted. Entering would prove dangerous.

Looking over his shoulder Running Horse waited to hear their decision. Nothing was said, but each gave a nod. So turning, the Indian swept away the cobwebs and entered. The others followed.

The old steps were steep. Single file the four descended; Running Horse in front with the candelabra, then Bowdie, then Riley and Daniel at the rear. The steps creaked and often buckled beneath their weight. With each step they feared the entire stairway might give way and send them plummeting to their deaths. Exactly fourteen minutes from starting down, they reached its end and stepped onto a floor of stone.

Daniel guessed the descent had taken them three hundred feet into the earth. They stood in a small room chiseled out of solid rock. The candle light shadowed the entrance of a narrow tunnel across the way, and inches above it hung an old board on which someone had carved words.

Moving to it Running Horse raised the candelabra and brushed away a layer of dust. The words were in Spanish.

"Tis dandy," Daniel said, "now we have no way of knowing what it's sayin'."

Riley spoke up, "Yes we do. I've had three years of Spanish."

Through the shadowy light Daniel smiled at Riley. "Riley McCaden," he said, "tis the McCaden of McCadens you are."

Riley smiled then turned and interpreted the words out loud: *These are tunnels of Evil. They are cursed. If entered they will be your end! I hid them beneath this house of God and prayed they would never be found. Turn and go back! If you do not, may God have mercy on your soul.*

Coronado

April, 3, 1541

Bowdie did the math. "Wow! Coronado hung this sign back in 1541. This church was built in 1797; that's two-hundred and fifty-six years after the Spanish Explorer's discovering. Someone years afterward, must have discovered the secret and built this big church over top of whatever it was Coronado had put up.

"Yeah," Riley said thoughtfully, "whoever it was, wanted to make sure the cities were never to be found again.

"Yeah, and somewhere along the way," Bowdie injected, "a map must have been made and hidden away. Maybe it was Coronado himself who made it, just to be safe."

Running Horse shrugged, breaking up the historical debate.

"My friends we must talk no more. We must hurry. The one you call Frog may come anytime, and we must go to the cities, and there set a trap for him, take from him the map, turn him over to your law, then Daniel take you back with the map and you see your families again."

Running Horse took in a deep breath, adding, "Or, you have learned what the words of the Spanish Warrior said. It was a strong warning. Do you wish to turn back? We do not know what waits." What to do must be made by you two!"

Light from the candles flickered eerily throughout the small, hollowed room. Riley spoke for them both. "There really isn't a choice Running Horse. We have to go to the cities and wait." We really need that map." Bowdie gave a supportive nod. "That's true."

The Indian looked soberly at Daniel and gave a nod. "Then so it shall be." He turned and entered into the tunnel.

Fifty feet after entering, the passageway branched into a Y. Pausing, they discussed which way to go. It was Bowdie who decided. "Does it really matter?" he said, "Remember what your father told us, Running Horse. We had to trust, have faith. The way I see it, if we were shown how to get here, we'll be shown the way back, no matter how many turns we make."

Resting a hand on Bowdie's shoulder the Indian nodded, "You have spoken well, Bowdie Pager." Turning right, Running Horse again lead the way.

The tunnels were of solid rock. Whether they had been worn away through the work of nature or laboriously chiseled by the hand of Indian people, they did not know.

But endlessly the stone passageways twisted and turned. It was barely noticeable but consistently they angled downward, taking them deeper and deeper into the earth. And Bowdie had been right about trusting the spirit. Always there were turns and choices to make of which tunnel to take. Truly, if the Dancing Spirit did not aid them when it came time to rejoin the world above, they would die of thirst and starvation long before finding the way out.

In several locations they found skeletal remains of what were once Spanish Soldiers. All had been dressed in armor. Their helmets, vests and shields were now covered with rust, their once colorful uniforms tattered and shredded by centuries of deterioration. Swords, Spears and Axes were clutched tightly in their hands as if they had died fighting someone...or something.

Suddenly Running Horse stopped and raised a hand. "Look my friends. Do you see what I see?" For the first time since venturing in they saw light that wasn't theirs. Far down the tunnel it appeared little more than a speck; but it was light.

Eager they pressed on toward its source, all wondering the same thing, had they found the Seven Cities? The light grew with intensity as they closed the distance. Running Horse blew out the candles. They had become no longer needed.

When the tunnel ended they exited onto an enormous stone-sculpted platform. Obviously chiseled by the skilled hands of Indian stonemasons, the work was breathtaking. It was the image of a giant's forearm reaching out with its palm turned upward. It appeared to be some sort of observation point; below it, some source of intense bright light was radiating upward.

Following a quick glance at one another they moved down the forearm and onto the upturned hand, huge fingers bent up serving as a kind of safety fence. Cautiously inching their way to the tips of the chiseled fingers they stopped.

There, standing shoulder to shoulder, they found themselves speechless.

CHAPTER SIXTY-THREE

What lay before them was startling. A hundred feet below the ledge extending for half a mile, a city lay nestled within the basin of encircling rock cliffs. Three and four hundred feet in height, these cliffs were lush with greenery: a multitude of various plants, trees and flowers of incredible colors.

On the far end of the city a hundred-foot waterfall poured out of the rock cascading downward into a lake of emerald, green. The cities themselves consisted of single-story dwellings of shimmering Gold, their roofs covered with a bright orange-tile. Streets and sidewalks were laid with silver, door and window frames were trimmed with Turquoise, polished to a glittering shine.

Streetlamps of black marble aligned the walkways, their extending arms holding great chandeliers of dangling crystal and glowing candles; with their light so bright building fronts reflected off the streets of silver.

A channeled river, green as the lake, weaved its way through the city; and at various locations white marbled steps descend down into the water's edge. Riley imagined they'd been built to allow people access to the water for swimming and fun.

The Seven Cities of Cibola were a wondrous place, possessing a peacefulness that brought joy and calming to the soul. Pain and fighting and sadness probably did not exist here. And although they were seven cities with the appearance of one, this place was heaven on earth?

Riley pulled his lip between his teeth and began gnawing at it; a new thought had popped into his head. All over the cities, hundreds of chandeliers held burning candles. They brightened the cities as if a golden, warm sun sat overhead. But there were no people here. Although lush and beautiful, the streets were empty, the cities deserted. Who kept those candles burning?

Professor Hale's warning came back. The streets would be guarded by the Angels of Death. Could it be them who kept the lights burning? And could these Angels also be the ones responsible for the disappearance of the city's population?

Running Horse interrupted Riley's thoughts. "The Dancing Spirit has shown us favor. We have arrived before the man called Frog. But he will know we are here when he finds the broken locks. We must be ready. We will rest here on the stone hand, for it gives us a good view of the tunnel. And each of us will take a turn standing watch at the tunnel's exit, looking for light and listening for the sound of someone approaching. This person will then alert the others."

To the right of where the tunnel exited a wide stone stairway lead down into the cities below. One by one that's where they took their turn watching for Frog.

Daniel was the first, Running Horse second, Bowdie third and Riley last. It was 4:30 am when Riley began his turn. An hour into his watch he stood at the top of the stairs staring out over the seven cities, awestruck. They were so mystical. So beautiful.

The people who had once lived there must have been so very happy. Wars were unheard of and crime unknown, no smog or big city noises. No snow or thunder storms to create problems like flooding, icy roads, or loss of electricity. It would have been the perfect place to live, and he wished he could show it to his mom and dad. A smile appeared at the corners of his mouth. Maybe one day he would!

And he was amazed over the plant life. How could flowers and trees and such grow way down here beneath the earth with no sunlight? Then again, how does life deep beneath the ocean survive, living in an environment of total darkness, freezing temperatures and thousands of pounds of pressure per square inch pushing against their frail bodies? They had somehow adapted. That was how it must be here. In some way they…"

Something cold touched the back of Riley's neck and he stiffened. Frog moved his mouth close to his ear and whispered, "surprise turd face!" His breath smelled like a stale cigar. From the corner of his eye Riley glanced over at the others. They were all asleep.

"What say we take a stroll through the cities and do some shopping? I just hate shopping alone, don't you?" Frog grabbed Riley's collar and forced him down the stone stairway.

CHAPTER SIXTY-FOUR

At the bottom of the stairway there loomed an archway of gold. And poised atop its arc sat the crouching figure of a winged demon preparing for flight; its stone eyes staring at them.

Riley was sure the archway was the point of which they were not to pass. Once they moved beyond it, he would be going against the Dancing Spirit's warning.

Frog whirled suddenly to face the stone stairway; his gun pointed. Daniel froze on the last step. "Not so fast, Irishman," Frog said quickly, "you keep your distance, and we'll all get along fine. Me and the kid are taking a little look see through the cities. Anybody follows and bang, no more kid. Know what I mean?"

Daniel nodded. "I, get it ya' big bag a blubber, but why the lad? He's scared. Can't ya' see he's frightened enough to start cryin."

Riley frowned. He wasn't going to cry for Pete sake. Sure he was worried about the Angels, but crying? Did his great, great grandfather really think him such a coward? It was he himself who had said McCaden blood flowed in his veins?

Daniel bit at his lip attempting to reason with Frog. "Can't ya' see there's sometin' wrong here in this place. The cities look as if they'd been made by the hand of God Himself, but there aren't any people, they're all missin'. Ya' ot not be goin' in there, Frog. I tell ya' there is sometin' wrong!"

Frog shrugged. "Just means no body will be getting in the way."

Daniel tried again. "Well than, ya' brainless bundle of Cow Manure, take me instead of the lad. I can be helpin' ya carry things."

Frog laughed, "Can't do it Irishman. I hate kids and if I get frustrated I got somebody to slap around. I'd just have to shoot you. Now start backing up those stairs and stay at the top when you get there."

Realizing he had no choice, Daniel began climbing the steps backwards talking to Riley as he moved, "Tis okay to be scared Riley, and okay as well to cry. Don't be hesitatin' to use the red bandana tied about your neck, tears can blur your vision and ya' need to be watchful of things that might be gettin' in your way."

Frog looked down at Riley with a snicker, "Yeah, you little cowgirl," he said "Great, great grand-pappy is right; a snot-rag that size will hold a whole lot of tears for a big baby like you. And since we're on the subject, I love the rest of your outfit too: the pretty blue shirt, the Barbie jacket with dangling fringe, your little toddler Indian belt, and my personal favorite, the matching cowgirl hat and booties." Frog looked up at Daniel then back to Riley, "I'll bet Gramps even bought you pink panties for underwear." Frog made himself laughed out loud.

But Riley's jaws tightened. He appreciated the outfit great, great grandfather had bought him. And it had dawned on him, Daniel McCaden wasn't implying he was a crybaby at all, he was reminding him to use the red bandana when the angels of death came; reminding him without letting Frog know.

And besides, this oversized kid-hating Jackass had insulted his great, great grandfather for the last time. Glaring up into the fat man's face Riley prepared to tell him exactly what he thought; and his choice of words, like the donkey synonym, were not parent approved. But the words were snapped out of him. Frog tightened the grip on his collar and jerked him nearly off his feet. "Come on, sis." He said, "Let's go shopping."

Frog moved backward; gun pointed at Daniel. When far enough away he turned facing the cities and shoved Riley to the front. "Okay, sis," he said placing his gun back into its holster, "you've got the lead. I suggest you don't try anything stupid like making a run for it; I'm a fast draw and can guarantee my bullet will outrun your scrawny little Hoosier boy legs."

CHAPTER SIXTY-FIVE

Always keeping Riley ahead, Frog moved in and out of houses stealing all he could fit into his pockets and a leather tote bag he took from the first house.

Inside each of the buildings things lay neat and untouched, as if people still lived in them but had stepped out temporarily. There was no dust or dirt anywhere. Children's toys lay on the floor waiting to be played with. Food sat in dishes ready to eat, clothes hung waiting to be warn, jewelry and personal items lay about. There was nothing indicating the houses were abandoned, only the missing people. It made Riley uneasy, but it didn't bother Frog. He continued moving house to house stealing all he could carry.

They had traveled deep into the cities when Frog suddenly pulled Riley to a stop. The fat man stood staring at a building different than the others. With a frown he spoke aloud. "Now why wasn't this visible from the ledge overlooking the cities? It towers higher than all the others; must be some kind of optical illusion."

Riley stared at it too, remaining quiet. The building sent chills running down his spine. He wrestled with the urge to turn and run. An urge so strong, the probability of Frog shooting him in the back would have been worth the risk.

This building, unlike the others, was not made of gold or silver, or any other precious metal. This one had been constructed of ancient stone; now worn and cracked and consisting of darkened gaps – looking as if had been neglected for centuries.

And it stood two-stories, the highest elevation point in the cities. Why, Riley wondered, did all the others shine and glitter with such brightness, while this one reeked with… DEATH! Riley couldn't help it; that was the word that came to mind.

Perfectly centered on each wall of the building was a single rectangular hole; a dark opening where a window should have been. Riley thought of them as watchful eyes staring out over the cities.

Suddenly Riley's own eyes widened and there was no stopping the word that exploded from his mouth, "Shit!" Riley McCaden never talked like that, but the cause of this outburst was unstoppable. What he saw shook the very foundation of any hope he may have had of getting out of the cities alive. Those black holes, those dark watchful eyes had suddenly begun to glow. Something inside was awakening, coming to life.

Since that cold rainy morning he had first entered Murda Mansion in search for Bowdie, he had been constantly experiencing unbearable things, but now, this went beyond any fear he had yet faced; this was… the end!

Frog pulled his gun holding it tightly in his hand.

From the windows the light was growing brighter, and it began to swirl in circles drifting outward; it was gentle, like the soft touch a fan turned low. Frog started to say something but stopped; suddenly from somewhere inside the ancient building there arose the sound of singing; a choir, their voices beautiful but words distant, indistinguishable.

Frog shook his head in disbelief, and at the same instant flower petals began shooting out of the holes and upward, than floating slowly to the streets below. Riley watched astounded, feeling as if it were snowing.

The delicate petals fell in an array of colors: white, reds, oranges, blues, greens and yellows. And while it was all so beautiful, Riley stared with alarm, for the floating petals were not at all affected by the breeze, which he realized was steadily growing stronger.

The singing continued with increasing volume as if the choir inside the building was drawing closer, and the light was brightening with intensity. It all appeared as if a grand celebration were taking place. But Riley knew none of this was right. Something was going to happen, something so very not good. He knew he had to run, to make it to the arch.

Turning on the balls of his feet he told himself he could do it, he was fast. But he was too late. Frog grabbed his collar yelling into a now howling wind. "Forget it pumpkin. You're not going anywhere."

CHAPTER SIXTY-SIX

There was no escaping now. And a sudden realization dawned; two realizations actually. First, all of the candles in the chandeliers had been blown out by the wind. And now, apart from the strange light emitting from the old stone building, the Seven Cities of Cibola lay in a shadowy darkness.

The second thing he realized; and this was the worst. Because of Frog's selfish greed he was going to die right alongside of this crazy fat man, lose his life in this long-forgotten place so far from home. He was going to die in the Seven Cities of Cibola and remain forever; a pile of bones lost to Legend. He knew that to be true, for the words of the singing choir were now clearly heard; and although soothing as the voices of Heavenly Angels, because of Frog, there message was a death sentence.

The Map - the map

Surrender to us the map!

Quickly now – for the Angels come.

And once arrived – too late to run.

Lay it down oh mortal man.

Else die in darkness by their hands.

Frog shouted in selfish rage. "No. It's mine and I'm keeping it."

Riley looked up begging "Please Frog, listen to them. Lay it down."

"No," he shouted back above the wind, "if I don't return to Climers with it, he'll have me killed."

Riley yelled again, "I need it too Frog, I can't return home without it. But if you don't give it to them we'll die right here. Use your brain."

"Forget it you trash bag maggot," Frog said tightening his grip on Riley's collar, "it stays right here in my pocket."

"NO, it's wrong Frog, don't you see?" Riley continued pleading, "This place is sacred. It's holy ground. Give it to them."

Frog gritted his teeth, "Who are you to be telling me anyway, you little punk cowboy want-to-be. I'll leave them something alright, but it won't be the map. Raising his pistol Frog slammed the butt down hard against Riley's head. Pain and light exploded through his brain, and he buckled to his knees.

Frog let go of his collar and Riley fell sprawled onto his back. Unconsciousness rushed in quickly, but Riley fought it; he had to remain awake, at least long enough to cover his nose and mouth with the red Bandanna. Clumsily his fingers began inching toward it, it seemed miles away. His head spun wildly, the pain throbbed, and blood was seeping into his hair. He wanted to sleep.

His mind was drifting, clouding, where was that Bandanna? He had to cover his nose and mouth; it was his only chance. His life depended on it. Sleep was over taking him. Then he touched it.

Fingers barely workable he maneuvered it in place, and barely in time. His strength gave out and his arm dropped to the silver street on which he lay. As unconsciousness rushed to steal his last sense of awareness; blurry eyes caught trails of colored lights shooting out from the ancient building and into the darkness above.

His eyes closed and sleep came just as he felt the red Bandanna being ripped from his face; Frog must have known. "I need this more than you do, chump. Frog said, his voice fading... sounding a million miles away.

CHAPTER SIXTY-SEVEN

For an unknown amount of time Riley slept in that world of nonexistence. Not knowing if he were alive or dead. Perhaps he dreamed, maybe it was all just a dream: Frog, Professor Hale, Running Horse, great, great grandfather Daniel, 1888, the Time Machine, Casey, Climers and all the rest of it. And then again, maybe this was death.

Then Riley's eyes opened. It was dark and shadowy, and he was back on the ledge, the others were gathered around him. Sitting up slowly, feeling dizzy, he asked "I'm not dead?" On the top of his head, the spot where he had been struck throbbed and radiated with pain. Touching it he wrenched and asked, "How did I get here?"

"Twas' a miracle Lad" Daniel told him.

Running Horse, holding the lighted candelabra nodded, "That it was. You were delivered to us as a gift."

"What?" Riley asked puzzled.

"Yeah," Bowdie broke in with excitement. "It was D.Q. Cool."

Frowning with confusion Riley shook his head, "What is everyone talking about?"

"It was an Angel, Riley", Bowdie said "he carried you here. Flew you right up over the ledge and laid you down right here in front of us. Man, God is so cool. He rocks."

Riley made a face, "Common."

Daniel spoke up again, "Tis true, Riley. It really was an Angel who brought you to us. He also left a message for ya'; for you and Bowdie both."

"What message?" Riley asked eager to hear.

"He said you'll not be needin' the map."

"What did he mean? Why won't we need the map?"

Daniel shrugged. "He didn't say, lad. But he did warn us to be gettin' out. This place was goin' to be destroyed."

"Destroyed, how?"

Daniel shrugged. "We don't know."

Just then somewhere in the darkness of the cities came a loud rumbling. The rock platform beneath them trembled. Running Horse rose quickly to his feet, "Come my friends," he told the others, "we were just told how the cities will be destroyed. To live we must run."

They had barely entered the tunnel when a violent explosion shook everything, its force throwing them to the floor. Only feet away, the beautifully sculpted hand and arm began to break apart, crumbling in sections and crashing a hundred feet to the floor below.

Scrambling to their feet thy heard yet another sound; it was the thunderous roar of a great wave of rushing water. The face of the rock cliff, once host to the serene and beautiful water fall had weakened and burst, now releasing a thunderous flood of water crashing into the cities.

As fast as possible without causing the candles to blow out, they charged through the tunnels, hearts pounding, hopelessly lost with no way of knowing if they were going the right way. The candles were burning down quickly, soon there would be nothing left, and they would find themselves in total darkness. For them, their only hope was to have faith.

Constantly the tunnels rumbled and trembled. Often so strong they were forced to stop and wait for it to quiet. And their violent shaking grew with intensity, drawing steadily closer, as if it were chasing them.

Nearly an hour had passed when one struck so fiercely it caused a cave-in behind them throwing fragments of rock and billowy clouds of dust into their midst. It grew difficult to breath and around them the ceilings and walls cracked. Out of those cracks water began seeping through. Then came another powerful tremble and the cracks widened to the point water began pouring out, drenching them and quickly covering the tunnel floor.

In several locations cave-ins had nearly closed the passageway and they scrambled madly removing rock and debris for enough space to crawl over and continue on.

The candles were down to mere stubs by the time they found the room with the old stairway. Cheering, they started up at a run, charging two and three steps at a time. The rickety construction swayed madly, but there was no choice; they had to trust that it would not give way. Coming down the ancient stairway had taken them fourteen minutes, going up took only nine.

One by one they exited into the security of the room behind the Alter; then together quickly pushed the door closed. Shoulder to shoulder, backs leaned against it, they sighed catching their breath. But it wasn't over.

Beyond the door in the crumbling darkness, the rumbling grew worse. The old Mission shook fiercely, and they feared it might collapse on top of them. Paintings fell to the floor, walls split in some of the rooms, pieces of ceiling crashed down, statues tumbled and outside sections of stone fence were breaking apart.

For what seemed an eternity the earth shook and rumbled, settling and resettling, crumbling and exploding. Someone, perhaps God himself, was burying the Seven Cities of Cibola forever.

When it was finally over, and the earth fell calm they dared to look one last time behind the door. Dust puffed in a huge cloud as they pulled it open. Tons of stone and rubble lay piled level with the Mission floor.

Truly, Riley's Angel had spoken correctly. The Seven Cities of Cibola had been destroyed. Never again would the eyes of mankind look upon them.

A. ALEX COME'

CHAPTER SIXTY-EIGHT

During the quake their horses had run off, but luckily not far. When recovered they mounted and headed for Tucson. The last speck of daylight was disappearing when they stopped to make camp for the night. Daniel cooked beans and put over coffee. After dinner the four sat sipping a cup while lost to their own thoughts.

The desert was quiet and above their heads the night sky was filled with stars. Running Horse threw a small log on the fire and Riley watched it burn. It was a soft light that shadowed the area with a gentle easiness. The flames felt good, for the desert was growing chilly.

Taking his last swallow of coffee Riley set the cup down and stretched out on his back, resting his head against his saddle. Pulling his blanket around him he sighed, staring up into the night sky. In his head he tried recalling how many days they had been gone from home. His parents no doubt were worried sick. And he was sure the police had searched everywhere for them, even the old mansion. The question was, did they find Climers and the TT- V? Probably not, it had been well hidden behind the secret wall.

Between him and Bowdie they had been through a lot: kidnapped, held prisoner, traveled through time, journeyed by dream to a bazaar strange land, rode by horseback through the Arizona desert, slept under the stars like cowboys, made friends with an Indian warrior, road in a carriage with the old neck stretcher himself, visited real western towns, was rescued by an Angel, and most of all saw with their own eyes what was said to be only legend…The Seven Cities of Cibola.

Riley's eyes were growing heavy. Yawning, he reached up and covered his mouth with his hand. Sleep was on its way and he was thankful, he needed it and it felt good. Bowdie had made his bed beside him, so he looked over at his friend and smiled. "Goodnight Bowdie." He said sleepily.

Looking over, Bowdie yawned too, "Back at ya, pard." A few moments passed then Bowdie added. "You know what, Riley?"

"What?"

"It's cool being best friends."

"Yep," Riley said pulling his hat over his eyes, "cool it is."

Somewhere in desert a coyote raised its head and howled at the starry sky.

Then a second coyote followed. They too were probably best friends.

CHAPTER SIXTY-NINE

By 8:30 they were back in Tucson and had the horses returned. By 10:00 they stood at the train depot waiting to board. The train whistle blew three consecutive times and the conductor yelled, "All aboard."

Daniel extended his hand to the Indian and he took it. With a smile Running Horse told him, "It has been a hard journey, but one that has made us friends. Always will my lodge be open to you."

"I," Daniel told him, "tis' the same with me."

Each gave a nod. Releasing his grip Running Horse turned to Bowdie. "You Bowdie Pager," he said placing his hands on his shoulders, "you stood like a warrior during our time in Dyroma. You made me proud. I think when you grow older you will make a good chief. Perhaps you will rise to chief of this country. If that happens, you will make this land a better place. I know this is true for it is in my heart."

Turning to Riley than, Running Horse smiled warmly "Riley McCaden, when you return to your own time, remember always the things we did here. For in years to come the memory of them will mean more than all the gold within the Cities of Cibola. When we are young we live the adventures, but when the bones grow old and the skin wrinkles all that is left are their memories. Treasure them."

The conductor shouted, "Last call, all aboard." The whistle blew three loud blasts again and steam blew up from around the wheels.

Running Horse gave a final nod to Daniel then turned away and walked to his pony.

The three hurried into the passenger car and found a seat. The train jerked forward, steam blew up past the windows and smoke belched from the engine's stack; they were rolling out of Tucson.

Another blow of the whistle pierced their ears when Bowdie shouted, "LOOK!"

Turning, Daniel and Riley saw Running Horse galloping his pony beside the train at their open window; he was smiling. Moving to the window Riley and Bowdie smiled back tipping their hats - the cowboy's salute of respect. But the train was gathering speed to quickly and Running Horse could not keep up. Reining his pony to a stop, he sat sober, raising his hand as a final good-by. His heart felt sadness but also joy. For he knew the white man's Iron-Buffalo was taking his friends home.

Riley and Bowdie leaned from the window holding on to their hats and waving until Running Horse was out of sight. Returning to their seats they plopped down with long faces. Daniel smiled warmly, "You'll be missin' him some, lads, tis no doubt. He was a good man. But always, he'll be in your hearts."

The train took them to Denver. There they switched to another, and it carried them to Saint Louis. Because of a long delay, they purchased tickets for a stagecoach and bounced their way to Springfield, Illinois. From Springfield a final train ride took them to Chicago and then straight into Lafayette.

The entire trip took nearly eight days of riding and waiting. They were tired upon reaching home and the familiar house looked like a Palace. Filled with joy Marie cooked them a thanksgiving dinner the following day.

According to the calendar it was July 19h. The TT-V was due to return in three days. The boys spent the time helping in Daniel's store, fishing the Wabash River with cane poles and touring Purdue University by horseback. The Purdue of 1888 was a cultural shock: nine buildings standing in the center of open cornfields. And State Street going up the hill from what was to become Wabash Landing was a white picket fence straddling both sides of that narrow dirt road they had spotted from the Covered Bridge , a long white picket fence stretching down both sides of the dirt road, from Chauncy long on past the nine buildings of the then Purdue University.

And on July 20th, both got to ride on one of the first to be used new City Electrified Street Cars. They road from Lair Hotel through down town, past Trinity Medthodist Episcopal Church, built in 1869 and got off at Great Great Grandfathers business on main. To Riley and Bowdie the things around them still remained peculiar. However, they had to admit, it was no longer the Twilight Zone.

CHAPTER SEVENTY

On the eve of their return, Daniel and Marie announced they were taking the boys to a restaurant for a farewell dinner. When dressed and ready to leave, Riley watched Daniel walk to the foot of the stairway and wrap both hands around the large decorative wood ball atop the banister post. He turned it clockwise unscrewing it.

Following a dozen turns, he lifted it free exposing a small hollowed compartment in the top of the banister post. Riley was speechless. Daniel reached in and retrieved a small wooden box from which he removed cash money.

Riley had always imagined there being a secret compartment hidden somewhere in the old house. He had actually searched for one many times while staying with his Grandmother. Once, he had even tried removing the ball just as his great, great grandfather had done, but it never budged. Now he understood why. He had tried turning it counterclockwise, like you'd remove a screw.

Daniel McCaden had threaded it the opposite way, knowing if someone were to break in and suspect the banister as being a hiding place, they would more than likely try turning the ball counter-clockwise as well. Riley smiled: *priority, check the secret compartment as soon as you're home.*

With money in hand, they left for town clopping along in a buggy similar to Judge Murda's, but not as fancy. The restaurant was nice; surprisingly very modern. Plush carpeting covered the floors. Tables were draped with white linen and matching rolled napkins wrapped by Ivory rings. Candles glittered in the middle of each table and in a far corner of the dining area, a violinist played softly.

While giving the waiter their drink requests, Bowdie tried ordering a beer, but Marie and Daniel grinned, shaking their heads no. And when Bowdie tried worming his way out of it by convincing them he was only kidding, Riley grinned thinking of Running Horse.

He had said if Bowdie were ever to become the chief of this country he'd make it a better place. *Bowdie Pager in the white house, President of the United States*; Riley's grin turned into a smile, *if that does ever happen, Running Horse; he told his Indian friend in thought, be thankful you lived in 1888.*

CHAPTER SEVENTY-ONE

6:30pm found them safely in the basement of Murda Mansion. Marie held a single candle and they sat huddled within its gloomy shadows. Casey had said the Machine would return at 7:30. This, Riley knew, would prove to be the longest hour of his and Bowdie's lives.

But at 7:16 they heard the first sound other than their own soft whispers. It came from the far section of the basement. Immediately Marie blew out the candle. Darkness came instant. They fought to quiet their breathing. The noise, whatever it was, grew louder and in no uncertain terms moved steadily in their direction. Then they saw the dim glow of a light.

Who could it be? Certainly not Frog, he was drowned and buried beneath tons of rock and rubble back in Arizona. Murda maybe, perhaps he had heard them, or witnessed their slipping in and was coming now with police to have them arrested. Riley closed his eyes: *just their luck. Arrested by the Old Neck Stretcher himself, on the very night the TT-V was to take them home.*

Whoever it was, the light grew brighter and brighter. The four pressed themselves tight against the wall, struggling not to be seen, praying the shadows kept them concealed. Then the person was there and stopped. They raised a lantern above their head, and it showed their face.

Bowie gasped and they whirled quickly, a gun in their hand. There came a snicker followed by the disgusting reptilian voice. "Well, look at this. Hail, hail, the gangs all here. Surprise, I ain't dead are you?"

Daniel, Riley and Bowdie stared with disbelief. Frog was in fact alive, but a mess. He was covered with dirt and dust, his suite tattered and torn, eyes puffy from lack of sleep, he was in bad need of a shave and cuts and bruises covered his face and hands.

The fat man forced a smile, "It was mighty thoughtful to come by and see me off." He glanced at his watch. "The Machine will be here in two minutes. But then, obviously you already knew that. It must have been Casey who told you." Shrugging he added, "no matter. When I get back and inform Climers, it'll be the last thing he tells anyone."

Riley spoke quickly, "You leave Casey alone. He's a good person."

Frog laughed. "Stop, you're scaring me again. And oh yeah," he said setting the lantern on the floor, "I still have it." He pulled the map from his pocket and waved it in the air.

Suddenly in the center of the room a tiny speck of blue light appeared. The machine was returning! Section by section the TT- V reconstructed, its timing impeccable. At exactly 7:30 it had materialized completely, spinning to a gradual stop with its red and blue lights aglow.

The instant it quit spinning, Frog approached the small door while holding his gun on the others. He spun the wheel rapidly and the door unlocked with a click. Opening it he told them, "Well I guess this is it, time to say good-by…permanently."

Bowdie's eyes were snapping with anger. He stepped forward and started to give Frog both fingers but changed his mind. This fat, selfish, kid-hating oddball deserved a much more extravagant farewell. Spinning, he turned his back to Frog, unbuckled his belt and dropped his jeans. Bending, he grabbed the elastic band of his underwear, but Riley stopped him; "For crying out loud Bowdie, not in front of my great, great grandparents." Bowdie froze, staring up into the shadowy faces of Daniel and Marie; both were speechless. Slowly straightening, he pulled up his jeans and buckled his belt, "Sorry, Mr. and Mrs. McCaden."

Frog was shaking his head, "you know I'm not going to miss you two butt-wipes one little bit. And to prove it, I think I'll leave the old Judge a little token of my appreciation for letting me use his basement. I'll leave him four dead bodies."

Frog pulled back the hammer of his pistol. That's when the voice came from inside the TT-V. "I don't think so."

Startled, Frog spun to look, but it was too late. Someone came hurdling out through the small opening tackling the fat man. They crashed hard to the ground and there began a deadly struggle. In the dim light Riley saw who it was and shouted… "DAD!"

CHAPTER SEVENTY-TWO

The two men rolled twice coming to a stop with Frog on top. Riley's dad was clutching the wrist holding the gun. Frog threw a punch striking Riley's dad in the temple. Although he felt its sting and it caused his ears to ring, he threw one of his own, connecting to Frog's chin. The big man moaned as he toppled free of Riley's dad.

Both scrambled to their feet and charged into one another with great force. Riley's dad was once again gripping the wrist holding the gun. They shuffled; turning and pushing, each struggling to maintain balance. Dirt swirled around them just as it had with the two fighters in Tucson.

Suddenly they tripped slamming hard to the floor; the gun went off with its bullet tearing into the wall just above Daniel's head. Its loud discharge raced off through the basement.

The struggle continued with Daniel not daring to get near for fear of getting himself or Riley's dad accidentally shot. Again the gun went off, this time the bullet zinging past Bowdie's ear. Riley's dad threw another punch catching Frog across the left ear. It didn't seem to faze him. He threw another, an uppercut hard beneath the jaw again. It worked. Frog was sent tumbling once more.

But this time the fat man rolled once and before Riley's dad could get to him, Frog leveled his pistol for a clear shot to the chest. And only a second before he pulled the trigger Daniel was there kicking the weapon free of the fat man's hand. It arched into the air and when it came down Daniel caught it. Frog looked on with surprise. The fight was over. Realizing he'd lost, Frog climbed to his feet raising his hands.

"Tis' over ya' blubber bag," Daniel told him as he approached Frog with the gun pointed. After pulling the map from Frog's pocket he motioned with the gun barrel, "Get over there and be huggin' the wall. I'll not be sayin' it twice."

Frog backed to the wall keeping his hands high.

Back on his feet Riley's dad gave Daniel a thankful nod; he had saved his life. Daniel winked, then walked to the Lantern sitting on the floor near the time machine's door. Looking at Riley's dad he asked, "Will ya' be needin' this?" Riley's dad shook his head with a positive no! Daniel than touched the end of the map to the lamps open chimney top. The heat quickly set it ablaze.

Daniel dropped it to the dirt floor just as the last sliver of paper curled black and died away. And so there it was an old map once worth trillions, a piece of paper the boys had risked their lives to possess, now nothing more than a pile of worthless ash.

Running into his father's arms Riley sighed, hugging him tightly. Squeezing him back, Riley's dad closed his eyes and smiled with thankfulness. He then released Riley and turned to Daniel, extending his hand. "You are my Great grandfather, Daniel McCaden, I presume?"

Daniel took his hand. "I. And you'll be my great grandson, Riley's father."

Riley's dad smiled. "Yes. Kevin McCaden." Releasing Daniel's hand, Kevin told him, "You have a grandson, and a great, great grandson who owe you much. Thank You."

Daniel smiled warmly. "No Kevin McCaden, tis no owin' anything, we're family." Then Daniel introduced him to Marie. And while Kevin gave her a hug, Frog made a wild dash for the darkness of the basement. Kevin turned to run after him, but Daniel grabbed his shoulder. "No need. It'll be him who is left behind now; suitable punishment for what he's done."

Behind them the lights of the TT-V made a clicking sound and switched from a steady glow, to flashing. There came another noise like the whining of an engine, and they knew the machine was getting ready to return.

"Quick boys," Riley's dad said, "we have to get aboard, or it will leave without us." Turning to Daniel one more time, Kevin smiled and the two embraced, than Kevin hugged Marie again and walked to the Machine's door to wait, allowing the two a moment with the boys.

Daniel stretched out his hand and Bowdie took it. "Bowdie," he said, "twas nice havin' met ya'. Normally I'd say come back and see us, but you'll be livin' much too far away for that. So God be with ya' and good luck in the future."

He then turned to Riley. Riley was crying. Knelling Daniel reached out and wiped a tear from his cheek then took him into his arms. "No need to be cryin' great, great grandson. Remember what Running Horse said to ya', that you'll always have your memories, and they're more precious than gold. I'll always love ya' Riley McCaden, ya' hang on to that."

The Machine was beginning to spin. Marie gave them both a hug and a kiss, than wiped away tears of her own. Riley's father yelled. "Sorry boys, there's no more time." They dashed to the machine and while running beside it, hopped through the opening. The last thing Riley saw of his great, great grandfather was him peering through the little window as he closed the door and spun the wheel.

Fighting to stay on his feet Riley's dad strapped them in, than did the same. The machine picked up speed, moving faster, shaking and vibrating. They strapped in quickly, shortly after, came the pain and darkness; they struggle to remain conscious. They felt the same sickness and light-headedness that seemed never to end. Around and around they spun… but this time they were going home. And after an unknown amount of time, the Machine began to slow and finally came to a stop.

Following a few seconds of regaining his senses, Riley removed the safety belt and stood slowly. His dad and Bowdie were still recovering. The wheel on the door was spinning; it was turning wildly. Someone wanted in. The final spin came, and the wheel stopped abruptly; the door clicked and immediately it was thrown open.

Riley didn't move. Dressed in a black suit holding a semi-automatic weapon, a stranger appeared, ready to shoot. But he was there only a second then moved away. In his place Riley's mom appeared. "Mom!" Riley exclaimed. Bowdie's parents were there too, peering anxiously over her shoulder.

Riley scurried out quickly with Bowdie right behind. Then out came Riley's dad. And there, beside the TT-V, the machine that had started it all; it was over. They were home, family again, celebrating a joyous reunion; a reunion that had taken a little over a hundred and forty-years.

CHAPTER SEVENY-THREE

Outside the TT-V things were different. There was no work crew in white smocks, no Harvey or Mr. Climers; only four men in black suits surrounding the machine standing well-armed, rigid and hard faced.

Then Riley and Bowdie saw Casey sitting in the kitchen sipping coffee. He was watching them. They waved and the old man raised his cup with a smile and a nod. He was happy they were safe, but he was also wearing handcuffs. Riley and Bowdie were instantly angry. Storming off for the kitchen one of the men in black stepped in front of the door shaking his head. Casey gave a wink as a means of explaining it was okay.

That didn't help. There was no way Casey deserved this kind of treatment. Without him they'd have never made it home. Their suspicions rising, Riley and Bowdie wondered what was going on. Wondering if these people were the CIA; if so, then where was Climers? He should be the one in cuffs, not Casey.

The move for the kitchen triggered the end of their time in the basement. Two of the men in black escorted them all outside and detained them there until a briefing with their supervisor.

The night was warm, and the sky glittered with stars. The white-gray light of a full moon shimmered bright off four black government cars sitting in front of the mansion's entrance. A half dozen other men in suits were roaming about.

Then out of the shadows came a short man built and bald like Frog, and he was smoking a cigar. The resemblance was eerie, and Riley and Bowdie caught their breath. But when he talked, his voice was not reptilian, so they sighed with relief.

The meeting was brief, warning them not to speak to anyone of what had happened or what they had seen. The parents acknowledged and turned to leave but Riley and Bowdie didn't budge. Looking into the shadowy face of the man in charge, Riley asked: "Harvey and Mr. Climers aren't here. Where are they?"

Pulling the cigar from his mouth the man in charge glanced at the stunned parents, then back to Riley, "Son, I have no idea who you are talking about."

Bowdie stepped forward, "That's Bull. I suppose you don't know a man named Frog, either?"

Pulling his gaze to Bowdie, the pudgy cigar smoker stared a long while at him, although he said nothing. Then suddenly he shifted focus back to the parents, "Go home. This never happened. And in the interest of the security of the United States, and your personal welfare, if questioned by the media or anyone else, you will deny everything. Need I say anymore?"

Nodding their acknowledgment, the parents briskly pointed the boys in the direction of home and began walking away. But Bowdie stopped one last time and turned to the Frog-looking supervisor, "Casey saved our lives. Without him we'd be dead."

"Yeah," Riley said angrily, "already dead a hundred and forty-years."

"Let Casey go." Bowdie demanded.

Riley didn't get a chance to reinforce Bowdie's request.

Spinning the boys around the parents hurried them away, marching through the woods toward the housing project and home; down the same path the boy's had taken by buggy ride with Judge Murda himself.

When they exited the trees, the housing project lay glittering in the moonlight. They smiled. To them it looked every bit as beautiful as the Seven Cities of Cibola. And they both imagined the same thing: a long warm running shower, a refrigerator filled with food. And best of all, the quiet security of their own rooms.

CHAPTER SEVENTY-FOUR

The next morning following a good home cooked breakfast, Riley insisted his dad drive him to his great, great grandfather's house...*his grandmother's house now.*

When they walked through the front door Riley paused, remembering the way it had looked in 1888. In his heart, he saw them all sitting their together: he, Bowdie, Marie, and Daniel; all drinking tea and eating chocolate cake.

Delighted God had brought her grandson home safely, his Grandmother hobbled to the doorway with a kiss and a loving hug. Riley returned them and gave her a smile, "It's great to see you again too, Grandma."

Then leaving her side he walked to the stairway banister and paused. Following a quick look back at his dad and grandmother, he placed his hands around the big wooden ball and sighed.

Then, with effort, Riley McCaden re-opened what had been closed well over a hundred and some years. In seconds he lifted the ball away; and there in the hollowed space sat the same wooden box, now old and covered with cobwebs.

His dad and grandmother watched in silent amazement. Riley pulled the box free and opened it. There was no money now, but in it he found various papers that had once belonged to Daniel and Marie.

There was also an old newspaper clipping telling of a thief sentenced to five years of hard labor by Judge Murda. The article had been headlined; **Frogman gets five years for breaking into Judges' house.** In some satisfying way, the story gave Riley a sense of closure. He couldn't wait to show it to Bowdie.

But it was the white envelope now yellowed with age and lying at the bottom of the box that surprised him most. It was addressed:

To Riley McCaden.

With a shaky hand Riley opened it and pulled out a letter. Sitting on the steps of the stairs, he unfolded it and read the words quietly to himself as he chewed on his lip.

My dear great, great grandson, by the time you read this, we will have been many years gone. I just wanted to tell you that in the years following your return home, you were always in our hearts and thoughts. And the telling of our great adventure has thrilled my children many times over. Where would we be without our memories? I did so cherish them! Please give our regards to Bowdie and your mother and father. Always remember I love you dearly.

Great, great grandfather Daniel

Riley's eyes filled with tears. Refolding the letter he placed it back into the envelope and wiped at his eyes. Then softly he smiled and whispered: "I love you too."

www.ingramcontent.com/pod-product-compliance
Lightning Source LLC
Chambersburg PA
CBHW040902010826
48978CB00013BB/1121